F   **Paisley, Linda**
             Hunter's Vigil

D1739097

HUNTER'S VIGIL

Other books by Linda L. Paisley:

Back in Eden
Jenny's Texas Cowboy

HUNTER'S VIGIL

•

Linda L. Paisley

AVALON BOOKS
NEW YORK

PRINTED IN THE UNITED STATES OF AMERICA
ON ACID-FREE PAPER
BY HADDON CRAFTSMEN, BLOOMSBURG, PENNSYLVANIA

In appreciation:

Sincere thanks to Rob Brooks of ROBrooks Custom Leather Shop, Bozeman, Montana, for his advice; to Amy Pearson of Clear Lake, Iowa, for her research; and to Dave Munsick of Dayton, Wyoming, for his inspiring music.

Chapter One

The big gray moved easily down off the rocky ridge, despite the size of the man on his back, and walked slowly forward. Smelling the water ahead, he whinnied and broke into a lope.

Hunter Grissom laughed. "I guess you're thirsty, boy," he said to his horse as they covered the remaining hundred yards to a spring. The water bubbled from the base of an outcropping of rock, making a small pool before its excess was funneled into a stream. Hunter reined in the gray beside the stream to allow him a drink of the cool, clear liquid.

The man dismounted and walked toward the spring. Checking on its condition was one of his planned stops that day, as he toured the wide expanse of his ranch. Seeing that the flow was normal and unobstructed, he stooped to replace a few rocks that had been scattered away from the edge of the pool. The rocks had been placed there years before to hinder erosion. He assumed some wild animals had watered recently and knocked them aside.

Hunter felt the ranch was fortunate to have this steady-flowing spring. It was a clean source of water for the livestock, and when his father had run the ranch, he'd had a

1

small dam built to form a pond near the ranch buildings. It formed an accessible reservoir in case of fire, and the fire danger was high this year. It had been hot and dry, little rain had fallen since June, and it was now nearing mid-August.

He rose and removed his broad-brimmed tan hat, then swiped a denim shirtsleeve over his damp forehead. He had a cowboy's tan: forearms, hands, neck and face had felt the touch of the sun, but his upper forehead was pale from wearing his hat low over his eyes. Underneath his hat, his hair was coal-black, thick and neatly trimmed, but with an almost permanent crease circling his head from the pressure of the band. Hunter had hazel eyes with crinkle lines at the corners, the result of many days of squinting against the sun and weather. His sturdy body stretched to over six feet. A five o'clock shadow darkened his jawline, even though it was barely two in the afternoon.

The gray's interest had moved from the water to the grass alongside the streambed. It was greener and taller there, not like the brown, heat-seared vegetation that now covered much of the lower pastureland. Hunter swung back into the saddle, taking a moment to glance at the blue, cloudless sky. Not a hint of a rain cloud in sight. Hunter sighed; it was one of those summers that he felt lucky to have made two good cuttings of hay, let alone three. He wouldn't have that much if he hadn't irrigated the south hayfield. There weren't as many bales stored in the hay barn for the coming winter as he would have liked.

"Probably'll have to buy some this winter," he muttered to himself, as he nudged his horse forward. He rode steadily to the south, crossed Clear Creek which was fed by the stream, and climbed through the mix of cottonwood, aspen, and willow trees to the meadow on the other side. He especially liked that area of the ranch and often rode there for pleasure, but today, he was busy checking fences and looking for anything out of the ordinary.

Several ranchers in the area had reported the loss of cattle over the past year. Pringle, his nearest neighbor, had missed eighteen head last autumn, not long before he would have taken them to market. A big loss monetarily for any rancher. Davidson of the Ruby Ranch had missed over forty head taken from a pasture less than a mile from his ranch buildings last spring. The latest disappearance had occurred at the Leaning Pine Ranch and involved about thirty head.

So far, the Grissoms of the Big G Cattle Company had been spared, but Hunter wondered how long their good fortune would hold. The cattle rustlers had been clever. There'd been no evidence left behind to point to anyone. All tracks—whether horse, motorcycle, or truck—had been cleared away, and considering the size of the landholdings in the area, often the losses weren't discovered for days or even weeks. By that time nature had also helped erase any useful evidence.

Thus, Hunter had increased his own inspection rounds and overall vigilance, as well as hiring more hands to watch over the summer range on the Forest Service lands he leased. The cowhands grumbled about being away from their more comfortable beds in the bunkhouse, but Clarence Bern, known to the cowboys as Cookie, had appeased them by volunteering to go along and set up a cook camp.

Hunter figured that hiring and feeding more men would be worth the expense, if they managed to keep him from losing cattle. Perhaps they would get lucky and catch the rustlers in the act, or at least get a lead on who was responsible.

"Blasted thieves!" he said vehemently, causing his gray to twitch his ears and look back at him. "Sorry, old fellow. I didn't mean *you'd* done anything wrong." He patted the horse's neck and slowed as they neared the end of the five-strand barbed wire fence, where it joined Pringle's land to the south at the top of a rise.

The Montana wind, as usual, was blowing steadily that

day. It hummed through the tautly-drawn wires. For Hunter, the sound brought back memories of a young woman singing and strumming a guitar as she sat on his front porch. Cathy had had a lovely voice and a talent for songwriting. She'd also had big dreams that hadn't included marrying a rancher.

Hunter shook his head and tried to lose the sound of Cathy's voice. It did him no good to think of her, and it always brought to mind his brother, Hale. He'd had big dreams, too. Hunter didn't know which person had caused him more distress, the girl he'd once hoped to marry, or the younger brother who had turned his back on the family and run off ten years earlier. Hunter sighed and turned the gray to move along the fence. He planned to cover the fencerow to where it met the federal land, then turn north.

Four hours later, he returned to the barns and turned the gray over to Ike Greene. The older man had worked for his father, Tom Grissom, from the day he bought the ranch. Then he'd been tophand; now in his late sixties, he was content to stay close and leave the herding and roundups to the younger men. Hunter had put him in charge of the ranch's horses, and Ike had proven very efficient at maintaining both their health and order in his horse barn, corral, and tackroom.

As Hunter hung his favorite saddle back in its place and returned his rifle to the locked rack in the tackroom, Ike mentioned that Cinnamon, a beautiful mare of that lovely shade, had a sore leg.

"It's a good thing I held her back and didn't let anyone take her up to summer pasture last month. I thought she was favoring one leg off and on."

"Think she needs Doc Bowen, Ike? If you do, I'll leave the call to you."

"Yeah, she hasn't responded to the liniment I put on her leg, so I'll call the vet."

"Okay, go ahead. I've got to get up to the house. Mom's

probably holding supper, and I've got a school board meeting tonight." He hurried down the aisle of the horse barn, then turned at the door.

"Goodnight, Ike," he called with a wide grin.

"Night, Hunter." The old man stood and stared at the door his boss had just passed through. *I wish that boy'd find himself a wife and start a new generation on this place. Tom wanted the ranch to stay in the family forever, he was so proud of what he'd built here, but, with Hunter unmarried and Hale off somewhere, that may never happen.*

"It'd be a blasted shame," Ike mumbled, as he turned to the phone in the tackroom to place a call to the vet.

In the house, Hunter washed his hands at the kitchen sink before he sat down in his usual place at the round oak table. His mother, Elizabeth, set a plate of homemade beef stew on the red placemat before him.

"It's about time you came in for supper," she chided, as she placed a basket of hot fluffy biscuits on the table and poured coffee for both of them. She sat across from him, folded her hands for grace, and murmured "amen" when her son finished speaking.

Elizabeth was tall with a womanly figure. She was proud of her still fairly slender waist. Hunter's black hair and hazel eyes came from her, as well as his name. Her maiden name was Hunter, and she came from sturdy pioneer stock, as her paternal grandparents had homesteaded in eastern Montana.

"I rode more miles of fence than usual today and checked the spring, too."

"How is everything?" she asked as she buttered a biscuit.

"No breaks in the fences. The spring is running normally, for this time of year. No sign of anything out of the ordinary."

"Well, that's good to hear." She sighed, then added, "I hope our luck lasts, and whoever's taking cattle stays away from our place."

Hunter smiled across the table at her frowning face. "Don't worry, Mom. With the extra hands on the herd, I'm confident we'll be safe." His smile said he meant it, but he crossed his fingers under the table.

His mother didn't share his attitude. She remembered when they'd lost some good cows to rustlers only a few short years after getting established on the ranch. It had made for a lean winter, financially; Tom had been very disheartened. Hunter had been only a baby then.

"I guess I'll take your word for it, son." She finished her stew and offered Hunter a second helping, which he took.

"This is good, Mom."

"Of course!" she chuckled. "This is board meeting night too, but you have time to make it."

"Yes, I'll finish this, take a quick shower, and head over there." He looked glum. "It'll probably be a complete waste of time though. I can't imagine a young, single woman wanting to bury herself out here in a one-room school. It'd be pretty lonely for her."

"Well, you said she had the proper credentials, and maybe she has the temperament to handle it. She can't be any worse than last year's teacher."

Elizabeth referred to a young man, fresh out of college, who had buckled under the solitude of rural Montana. He had wanted out of his contract, but he agreed to honor it in exchange for a good reference toward his next job.

"He did just fine with the subject matter though, and the kids liked him," Hunter said, as he pushed back his chair. "Well, I'll know in a few hours if we have a teacher for this fall. I hope so. I'd hate to have to start the process over again at this late date." He rose and climbed the back stairs that led up from the kitchen.

Hannah Morgan looked nervously about, though she tried not to show her anxiety. She had just stepped through the door into the passenger reception area of the airport. She knew she was to be met, but she had no idea by whom.

A sense of relief filled her when she saw her name on a piece of paper held by a pleasant-looking white-haired woman. Hannah smiled and walked toward her.

"Hello, I'm Hannah Morgan." She extended her hand, and the lady, who introduced herself as Beatrice Davidson, shook it.

"So glad to meet you, Ms. Morgan. Welcome to Montana."

Hannah thanked her. Then Bea, as she requested to be called, led her to the luggage collection area. When they had picked up her lone bag, they exited the airport into the sunshine of a hot day.

Bea put on sunglasses. "If you decide to take the teaching position, Hannah, you may need a pair of these," she said, as she tapped their frame. "It's been a very warm, dry summer this year."

Hannah smiled. "I've a pair with me, Bea. It's been very hot and dry in Kansas too."

They stowed the bag and Hannah's carry-on in the back of Bea's minivan and left the airport grounds.

"Now I'm going to drive into Bozeman so you can see a little of the city. It has a lot of places to shop, and many people from our area make the drive over occasionally. The university is here too."

Bea continued to talk and point out things of interest, then left the city on a highway that led toward Turk. Hannah thought it a beautiful drive and told Bea so.

"I think so," Bea agreed with a smile. "Now Turk is small, but it's where some of us go for groceries and such. It's also where our students attend high school. It's a long bus ride for them, which is one of the reasons our ranching community of Whetstone has worked hard to keep our little school operating. We think it better to keep our younger students closer to home."

"I see your point, Bea. It'd make a terribly long day for the young students. Rather long, even, for the high schoolers." She paused, then added, "Since becoming interested in this job opening, I've been reading about one-room schools and discovered that there are still many in Montana. The vast distances seem to be the predominant reason."

"Yes, I'd say so, that and community-mindedness. The board will be impressed that you've read up on Montana and our type of school. Be sure to mention it."

Hannah asked: "Exactly where is the job interview, Bea? Will you be able to drive me there?"

"Of course, dear. It's not until eight o'clock, so we have plenty of time. I'm the Board Secretary, so I'll be there to introduce you. In the meantime, we'll go to my home and you can unpack before we have supper."

"Thank you, Bea. You're very kind. I really think I'd enjoy the experience of a one-room school, and Montana itself is certainly appealing." Hannah peered at the rugged peaks in the distance. "Those mountains are just beautiful."

"That they are, but I'll warn you that the winters can be very frigid. A lot of snow, blizzard conditions, high winds—not that I'm trying to discourage you." She laughed. "But, I guess we're mostly hardy souls out here and just keep going about our business."

Despite the winter conditions, Hannah assumed.

In the bedroom that had belonged to Bea's married daughter, Hannah looked at her reflection in a dresser mirror. She had changed from slacks and a light pullover cotton shirt, that had been comfortable on the plane, to the gray two-piece suit she often wore when the occasion demanded she look professional. This being one of those occasions, she had packed it.

Now she noticed how severe it seemed and was glad she'd added a soft blouse in a peach shade. She tucked a matching peach handkerchief into her breast pocket so that the folded tips showed, then touched up her makeup. Not one to wear much, as a rule, she felt it would add to the mature image she hoped to project. Brushing her brown hair back, she rolled it into a chignon and fastened it securely, thinking it would add to her hoped-for mature look. To her ensemble she added gold clip earrings and her serviceable wristwatch, then stepped into low-heeled dark-gray pumps. They added two inches to her five feet four inch height, and somehow that increased her confidence.

Picking up her purse and a folder that held a list of possible questions to ask the school board, she joined her hostess in the kitchen of the ranch house.

In a few minutes, they were driving to the school. As they passed through Whetstone, Bea commented, "This is Whetstone. Now don't blink, or you'll miss it."

Hannah laughed and agreed that it *was* tiny. It consisted of a small white church with a cemetery, no more than ten or twelve houses, and a store with gas pumps out front. Bea explained that a pastor came out from Turk every other Sunday, but that they held their own service on alternate Sundays.

"Most of the folks that live in town are retired ranchers and have no children of school age. But, some of them have grandchildren in school and are very supportive of its operation. The Whetstone Store is really a combination small grocery store and restaurant. It's also often used as a gathering place for retired folks and for local meetings."

"Who runs it?" asked Hannah. She was curious about such a unique small-town enterprise.

"Mary Jerome, with the help of her husband Jim. He's confined to a wheelchair now; a degenerative muscle condition. But, they manage to keep the business going. They have two grown sons that stop in when Mary needs their help, too."

Linda L. Paisley

Hannah was still thinking about the Jeromes when Bea turned left into a short gravel drive that led to the school-yard.

"As you can see, we're about a half-mile south of town. That'd be your house to the left, and the school to the right. It's a bit isolated. I hope that doesn't throw you off the idea of teaching here."

"No, not at all," Hannah replied, as she got out of the car and glanced around. Perfect, she thought happily, this is just perfect. The school was built of white clapboard. The teacher's house was newer and made of peeled logs. Aloud she exclaimed over the buildings and the site. "Oh, Bea, this is lovely. I wouldn't have imagined anything so solid-looking and attractive. I can't wait to see inside."

"Well, let's go in then. It's nearly time for the meeting to start."

Hannah nodded, smoothed her suit jacket over her hips, and took a deep breath. She followed Bea up a gravel path toward the schoolhouse door, which was under a small por-chroof. Inside, they entered an old-fashioned cloakroom lined on both sides with metal hooks for hanging coats. Above the hooks were storage shelves and below were wooden benches. They passed through another door into the schoolroom proper.

Hannah's eyes darted quickly around the large room as she took in as much detail as she could in one short glance. Her attention was then drawn to the men who sat on chairs drawn into a circle at the front of the room. One man sat at the teacher's desk. Bea walked toward them and Hannah followed.

The men stood politely, and Bea introduced her to them, moving around the circle.

"Hannah Morgan, this is Roy Pringle, Frank Regola, Chuck Carson, and Hunter Grissom, our Board Chairman."

Hannah shook hands with them in turn, as she made mental notes as to their identity in order to know them later.

Everyone appeared friendly. Mr. Pringle, a gray-bearded man, smiled broadly. Mr. Regola, a slightly-built blond, simply nodded, and Mr. Carson, a sandy-haired middle-aged man, welcomed her most effusively.

"I hope you like Whetstone, Montana, Ms. Morgan. You'd be a welcome addition to our little community."

"Thank you," she replied, and smiled charmingly around the circle. She then turned to the man behind the desk, who had been watching the others. For some reason, tension knotted in her stomach as she looked into his eyes.

Hunter Grissom was good-looking. She liked his black hair and pretty hazel eyes, but she didn't understand why they looked at her so coolly. He was taller than the other men, and she found that her need to look up at him disconcerted her. But she smiled warmly and extended her hand.

"How do you do, Mr. Grissom?"

He took it in his large hand. She felt tough, work-worn calluses press into her skin. It made her realize that her hands had gotten soft in recent years.

"Just fine, Ms. Morgan," he replied, releasing her hand. "Would you take a seat, please, and we'll begin."

Hannah sat on the empty chair next to Bea and mentally composed herself. She wanted the job, but she knew it wouldn't be the end of the world if she didn't get it.

Hunter had watched her enter the room and glance around. He wondered if she was disappointed at the sparsely-furnished classroom. Then he noticed how gracefully she crossed the room. The other board members certainly seemed to be charmed by her, but he had learned to beware of smiling, disarming females.

He cleared his throat and thanked her for travelling so far for the interview.

"My pleasure, Mr. Grissom." She sat up straight in her chair, made sure her knees weren't too exposed, and waited for his first question.

"Your resume tells us that you've taught for five years in Topeka, Kansas. No offense, but you look young for having gained that much experience."

He looked at her and awaited a response.

So much for projecting a mature image, Hannah thought, then replied, "I was fortunate to be able to enroll in college-level classes while still in high school. That and going to summer school allowed me to graduate early."

Mr. Regola suggested: "Sounds like you were eager to get started on your teaching career."

"Yes, I was. When a position was offered to me in the same school in which I'd done my practice teaching, I gladly accepted."

"I'm wondering why you're now looking for a change?" Hunter interjected.

"I've enjoyed the past five years very much, but I decided to leave Topeka for a year or so. Knowing that my credentials would also be honored in Montana, when I saw your opening listed on the Internet, I decided to look into it."

"Why a one-room school, Ms. Morgan? The atmosphere will be quite different from a big-city school." Hunter leaned back in the chair and folded his arms across his chest.

Hannah noted that sign of defensiveness and wondered why he felt that way.

"Yes, it will, but it'll also be a challenge. More lesson plans to prepare, but the opportunity to work individually with the pupils, as well. Since I became interested in the position, I've spent time learning about one-room schools and how to best meet the needs of the variety of ages and levels of competence."

Bea nodded and smiled, pleased that Hannah had gotten that into the interview. Bea wondered why Hunter Grissom looked so wary. She would have thought he'd be thrilled with the teaching candidate's enthusiasm and background.

"I think we should tell you that fourteen pupils are expected to be enrolled this school year," remarked Mr. Pringle.

Hunter cleared his throat and picked up a paper. "Yes, two first graders, two second level, three third, four fifth graders, two sixth, and one eighth grader. He'll go into Turk for high school after this year." He paused and looked directly at Hannah. "Does that seem manageable?"

She had the impression that he expected her to say no, but she firmed her resolve and replied, "Yes, quite manageable, Mr. Grissom. If I'm offered the position, I'll work hard to see that you, the rest of the Board, and the parents aren't disappointed."

"Miss Morgan," inserted Mr. Carson, "I think it only fair to warn you that a Montana winter can be long and harsh. Also, you may find the teachers accommodations rather isolated."

"Well," Hannah answered with a tiny smile, "winter in Kansas is often harsh too. As for the house, living in a log cabin rather appeals to me. As long as the locks are adequate, of course."

"Oh, they are, Ms. Morgan, they are," Hunter assured her.

She saw the brief flicker of a smile on his face. *Well, he can actually smile, and his face didn't crack!*

She suppressed a giggle at that wayward thought, then composed herself as Mr. Grissom read a general description of the curriculum, as approved by the office of the county's Superintendent of Schools.

Hannah listened intently, then accepted those sheets of paper and one on which had been typed her salary offer and other conditions of employment. She read it quickly. The salary was the amount advertised, and she was pleasantly surprised at the additional perks that accompanied the position.

She smiled, her glance encompassing the circle of people. "I'm pleased but surprised. I assumed that as part of my duties, I'd be expected to also clean the school and perhaps pay my own utilities at the house."

Mr. Pringle chuckled. "Well, we don't want to over-burden our teachers, Ms. Morgan. We pay a retired couple who live in Whetstone, Olive and George Bergman, to come in to clean twice a week. George will also see to snow removal and a wood supply."

"I'd noticed the stove. Is that the only source of heat?"

"No, both the school and house have electrical heating units, but considering the severity of our winters, in case of blackouts, we keep a good supply of chopped wood on hand," replied the board member.

Hunter added, "As to the house utility bills, they're on the same meter as the school. I think you'll find the house comfortable. It's basically furnished, but of course, feel free to bring any of your own things that you'd like."

"Of course." She looked more closely around the school-room. "I'm happy to see a piano available and the computers. It's good that you've connected to the world in that way. Any age child benefits from experience on a computer."

Mr. Carson smiled. "I think you'll find the children, especially the older ones, very computer literate. We realize the importance of preparing them, as much as possible, for their high school years."

Hannah was pleased to hear that. It seemed the Whetstone school board strived to provide the best atmosphere for learning and preparedness for their students' futures.

"Ms. Morgan, I'm sure you'd like to see the house before making a decision. Shall we take a break, and Bea can show you around," Hunter offered. He stood and reached into his jeans pocket and passed a set of keys to Bea.

Chapter Two

Everyone rose. Bea and the men, except Hunter, went outside. He took a few minutes to show Hannah around the rest of the building. At the adjoining computer desks, he pointed out the training and educational disks stored there.

"These are good choices, Mr. Grissom. Students learn more easily from learning disguised as game playing." She smiled up at him, which only seemed to make him look more somber. "Is the school online?"

"Yes, though problems sometimes occur. We're connected to a statewide educational system."

"That's good to hear. It'll be a wonderful source of information for the children."

She took a minute to try out the piano.

Hunter grimaced. "Uh, I'll see that it's tuned before school starts, Ms. Morgan."

"That would be appreciated, Mr. Grissom."

They next paused near bookshelves that comprised a library corner. "There's a bookmobile that comes out from Turk on alternate Wednesdays, and we usually budget a hundred dollars for new books each year, but last year's teacher didn't avail himself of it. So, if you see fit, please feel free to go over that limit."

Busily looking over the books, Hannah mentally noted some titles that she'd already like to add to the little library. "Yes, I will, thank you. I have a number of books that I could bring with me too. Would it be all right for me to make them available to the children?"

"Of course. Now over on this side of the room," he walked toward the corner near the front door, "we've put in a tiny kitchen."

Hannah saw a sink, small-scale refrigerator and range, plus a microwave. "How nice. Handy for storing lunches and heating them up, if needed. Maybe for an occasional cooking class, too."

"I imagine the students would like that idea very much, Ms. Morgan."

"I expect it'll be quite a full and busy schoolyear, that is if the board decides to hire me."

Hunter made no comment, only showed her the side by side restrooms near an inner door that led to a garage and storage area.

"No need for a lock here," he explained, as he lifted a wooden bar resting in iron brackets. "This should make you feel safer, when you're alone in the building. The shades on the windows will help too."

Hannah felt a bit chagrined, but answered, "Yes, both will. I hope I didn't come across as overly cautious, earlier. Being concerned about locks and all."

"No, Ms. Morgan, not at all. It's only sensible, considering you'll be living alone, and I haven't met a teacher yet who didn't stay late at his or her desk." He seemed to be lost in thought for a moment, then continued. "Are you sure you're willing to live out here? It's a half-mile into Whetstone."

Looking serious, Hannah replied, "I'm sure, Mr. Grissom. I'm not known for being a nervous sort, but I'm glad to know of the locks and that handy bar."

They stepped through the door into the garage.

"You can store your car in here. There's a plug-in for the engine block against those below-zero nights. As you can see, we stack the chopped wood here under cover, as well as some supplies, and the mower and snowblower George uses."

Hunter lifted the overhead garage door, and they walked out onto the driveway. Bea left the group to ask Hannah if she was ready to see the house. Hannah agreed, and they walked single file up the path to the log cabin.

The path climbed moderately, as the house was built on a rise to the north of the school. It was set among pine trees, and Hannah recognized several tall lilac bushes growing on either side of a wide porch.

Bea unlocked the front door and turned on an overhead light. She then stood back to allow Hannah to enter. The younger woman walked to the center of the room and turned in a circle, a delighted smile on her face.

"My goodness, Bea, this is very nice."

There were built-in bookshelves on either side of a stone fireplace. Facing the fireplace was a couch in a green and blue print with a matching chair and footstool. There were several tables and lamps, and the floor was made of highly-polished oak boards. Under a double window to the right of the front door sat a maple dining table with four chairs.

"I'm glad you like it, Hannah. Come see the kitchen."

It was a corner kitchen with seemingly adequate cupboard space in warm maple. There was an island work area with more storage space behind sliding doors.

"This is a nice touch, Bea. Very modern."

"Yes, Hunter added that about four years ago. He likes to keep the house attractive to our teachers."

"That's above and beyond the duty of a board chairman, isn't it?" Hannah asked, as Bea opened twin folding doors to reveal an apartment-sized stacked washer and dryer. The bathroom was next to them.

"Perhaps, but Hunter takes it seriously. You see, his father donated the land for the house many years ago, and he provided a major portion of the money needed to erect it. Of course, others pitched in as well, both financially and with physical labor. I believe that Hunter feels a responsibility to see that all is well with the property."

Hannah murmured "I see," then followed Bea up a narrow open staircase to a loft above the kitchen and bathroom areas. From a railing, you could look down into the living room. There was a large closet, a dresser and chest of drawers in dark pine, and a double bed. On the floor were several scatter rugs.

Hannah stooped to examine one. "Why, this looks handmade. It's beautifully done."

"Those, and the ones in the living room, were made by a local lady, old Mrs. Prentiss, who has her own loom. It's a hobby, but she sometimes sells them at arts and crafts shows. It was her donation to the teacher's house. You see, many gave of their time and talents, as well as money."

"I hope to meet her sometime." She and Bea returned to the downstairs.

"It just occured to me, Bea, Mr. Grissom must have attended this school. Does he now have children among those I'll be teaching?"

"Oh, no, dear. Hunter isn't married. Now, Roy Pringle has a grandson attending; Frank Regola has a daughter in the fifth grade, I believe; and Chuck Carson's the father of the lone eighth grader. My grandchildren live on the other side of Turk, close enough that they go to school there."

"Goodness, there's so much to learn. Not only about my pupils, but about the community." She looked slightly embarrassed. "I'm speaking out of turn. I haven't been hired yet."

"Personally, I think you favorably impressed the board, and I was already persuaded," Bea replied with a little laugh.

Bea switched off the lights, then locked the door behind

them. Rejoining the men, Hannah commented that the house was very nice, very cozy, and certainly had all the modern conveniences.

Hunter murmured that he was glad she liked it, then added, "While we've been talking unofficially, Bea should join us for the rest of the meeting. We'll try to be quick, Ms. Morgan. Do you mind waiting out here?"

"Of course not. I'll just sit here until you're ready for me." She sat down on a wooden bench at one side of the outer door and closed her eyes.

Well, it's decision-making time. I think they'll offer the position to me. Do I really want it? Yes, I do. These people are friendly, with perhaps the exception of Hunter Grissom. The solitude will give me time to think and write—and to heal. Yes, I do want it.

Inside, the board discussed her merits. They all felt she would develop a good rapport with both students and parents. They liked her five years experience and her enthusiasm.

Hunter posed a problem, as he saw it.

"I'm afraid the isolation will get to her in a few months. Last year's teacher didn't like it. Do you think she'll be able to handle it?"

"Well, Hunter," Bea proposed, "I suggest that you, as the unmarried person on this board, be appointed to check in on her. See that she has what she needs. You *could* provide her with a bit of a social life too. See that she meets people and learns where she can find things in the area. In a purely professional capacity, of course."

Bea returned to her note-taking, but with a sly smile on her pleasant face.

Hunter's mouth gaped. Chuck Carson laughed aloud, and the other men chuckled.

Hunter snapped his jaws shut. Bea Davidson was an old friend whom he liked very much, but he didn't like what she had just suggested.

He responded indignantly, "I won't have time for that, Bea. Perhaps *you* could take Ms. Morgan's social life under your maternal wing."

"Perhaps. Anyway, I move that we hire Ms. Morgan on the standard one-year contract. If that's okay with you, Hunter?"

"Yes," he grumbled, then in a more formal voice: "There's been a motion to hire Ms. Morgan for one year. Is there a second?"

"I second the motion," Roy Pringle said firmly.

"All in favor, raise your right hand," requested Hunter. "Madam Secretary, please note in the minutes that the vote was unanimous," he concluded. "Being closest to the door, Frank, would you call her in?"

He did so, and Hannah accepted their offer. The meeting adjourned soon after she was apprised of the date on which she would be expected to begin. At her question, the board agreed that she could move into the teacherage a week earlier to settle in, before she began her plans for the opening week of school.

Quite satisfied, Hannah shook their hands, thanking each of them in turn. Hunter again looked cool and a bit reserved. Bea and Hannah left to drive to the Ruby Ranch then the next morning, Bea put her on the plane back to Topeka.

After the meeting, Hunter enjoyed a piece of cherry pie and coffee with his mother in the kitchen of their home. Elizabeth was full of questions about the meeting.

"I'm glad it's settled. So, the other members approve of Ms. Morgan?"

"Yes, they were very taken with her. She does have excellent credentials, and she's experienced. They all felt she'd be liked by both the students and their parents."

Elizabeth raised an eyebrow. "You seem unsure, son. What's *your* opinion of her?"

Hunter took a swallow of coffee before he spoke. "In

general, I agree with them. But I'm still not convinced that she won't turn tail and run when winter closes in on her. I don't think she realizes how bad a Montana winter can be or how isolated it sometimes is."

"Perhaps we'll have a milder winter than normal."

"That's possible, of course." He took a bite of pie and slowly chewed it, then said, "Bea suggested a strange thing, Mom. She thinks I should become a one-man committee to look out for Ms. Morgan, being that I'm the only single member on the board. She even went so far as to propose that I see that the woman has a *social* life." His dour expression showed what he thought of Bea's idea.

His mother smiled. "Well, son, you know what a matchmaker Bea Davidson can be." She paused thoughtfully. "But, who knows, that may be a good idea."

"You're not serious! I don't have time for looking after her. Too much to do here on the ranch."

"But think about it. If you take her a few places and introduce her around, some other single man may become interested in her. That may lead to our keeping her as our teacher for more than one year."

Elizabeth secretly hoped he'd agree with her premise. Even better, Hunter could become interested in the young woman himself. She would dearly love having children in the house again.

"Is she attractive, son? What does she look like?"

Hunter glanced across the table, an eyebrow raised, as hers had been moments before.

"She's nice enough looking, I guess, though a bit on the plain side. Slender, about five feet four or five, sort of mousy brown hair. A little young looking, considering she's taught for five years, but she explained that she'd started college early. She had a nice walk, graceful, you might say, and her eyes are a kind of soft gray. I don't know. I didn't pay much attention to how she looked."

His mother almost choked on her coffee. *Sure you didn't,*

son. For not paying attention, he had just given a very full description of the young woman. Elizabeth wanted to chuckle, but held it back with a supreme effort.

"So, she's rather plain. Well, someone may still become interested in her, being that there's a lack of young, single women around here. She must be an intelligent girl to start college early, as you said."

Hunter seemed irritated. "I didn't mean she was *ugly,* just a bit plain. I suspect she doesn't work hard at being pretty, like some girls do."

"Well, teaching is a busy occupation too, like ranching. Not a lot of time to spend on herself, perhaps."

"That may be. You know, she handled herself well at the interview. She was personable and charming, but somehow, I sensed that she was making an effort. I think she's actually shy."

"That's interesting. You know, you've intrigued me. I'm looking forward to meeting this Hannah Morgan."

"Well, she'll be back in about ten days. She's driving out. Said she could pack all she'd need into her car. Thanks for the pie, Mom. I'm going up to bed."

"Goodnight, Hunter."

Elizabeth lingered a little longer at the table. She thought that she'd have to call Bea tomorrow. She was curious to hear Bea's impression of the young teacher. More importantly, she wanted to learn her opinion of how Hunter and Hannah Morgan had reacted to one another.

Hannah's arrival at her parents' home in Topeka had been bittersweet. While they accepted her reasons for moving, they said they'd miss her terribly. Hannah felt the same, but tried not to think about it. She filled the next week with sorting and packing her belongings. In order to close out her apartment, she planned to store a few items at her parents' house.

Boxes of books, her laptop, a small microwave, her CD

player and disks, TV, a VCR and collection of tapes, both educational and favorite movies, a selection of songbooks for the classroom, a cookbook for children, and other supplies were crammed—along with her clothes and personal items—into every spare inch of her four-wheel drive sport utility vehicle.

Hannah was grateful that she'd purchased such a useful mode of transportation when she began teaching. Now, the loan was paid off. That was good, since her Montana salary fell short of her Topeka wages.

Saying good-bye to her parents and younger sister had been hard.

"We all love you and wish you luck," her father said gruffly. "Phone and e-mail us often. We want to keep up with you and your activities."

"It just seems so far away, Hannah."

"Don't worry, Mom. I know I'm going to be happy there. The people are friendly, and you know how much I like the house and school. I'll keep in touch, I promise."

She hugged her mother and father, then her sister, Heidi, who had been standing to one side.

Heidi whispered in her ear, "I'm sorry, Hannah. Please forgive us and be happy out there."

"There's nothing to forgive, Heidi. It's just how things worked out. You promise me that you'll be happy too."

Heidi nodded and forced a small smile. "Bye, big sis. Please, be careful."

Hannah got into her car and waved at her family, took one last look at her childhood home and pulled away from the curb. Leaving them was more heart-wrenching than she'd thought it would be, but it was necessary under the circumstances. *Life is never simple.* She sighed and put a soothing CD into the dashboard player.

Four days later, Hannah was on the last leg of her journey to Whetstone, Montana.

After leaving Interstate 90 at Bozeman, she followed Bea's written instructions which took her through Turk. The route looked familiar as the miles passed.

"Let's see," she murmured to herself, "instead of going to the crossroads where we turned to the right to drive to Bea's place, the Ruby Ranch, I'm to watch for a lane on my left. The Big G Cattle Company. Impressive name for a property."

It dawned on her that the "G" stood for Grissom at about the same time she spotted the carved and painted wooden sign that arched on posts over the lane. Of course, it stands for Grissom, she thought to herself. I'm to stop here first to pick up the house and school keys from Hunter.

Turning left, she rumbled over a cattle guard, then drove slowly, wondering where in the world the house was.

She tried to think of Hunter as Mr. Grissom, as he was technically one of her employers. But Bea kept referring to him as Hunter, and now Hannah thought of him by his given name more often than not.

She drove a half-mile up the lane through pastureland before she crested a rise and saw the ranch buildings. All painted a pristine white, there were three barns, several smaller buildings, and a large two-story house with bright blue shutters on the many windows. The house was set among large cottonwoods and a few other trees Hannah couldn't name. To her right was definitely an orchard and, as she neared the house, she could also see a well-tended kitchen garden.

Hannah pulled into the barnyard and parked near a pickup truck bearing the logo of the Big G Cattle Company—a large "G" with a smaller "c" to each side of it. She got out, stretched her limbs, and smoothed her blue tanktop back into the waistband of her denim jeans. She followed a cement walk toward a screened-in back porch.

As she approached, the door opened and a smiling woman greeted her.

"Hello, you must be Ms. Morgan. I'm Elizabeth Grissom, Hunter's mother." She shook Hannah's hand warmly.

"I'm pleased to meet you, Mrs. Grissom. I hope I'm not stopping at an inconvenient time. My note from Bea—Mrs. Davidson—directed me to stop by your ranch for the keys to the house and school."

Hunter's mother was an attractive woman, in Hannah's opinion, and certainly friendly.

"It's never an inconvenient time for company, Ms. Morgan, especially when you live so far from your neighbors. Come inside out of the sun."

They crossed the porch into the kitchen. Elizabeth offered the use of the bathroom off the hall so that Hannah could freshen up.

"I know you may be anxious to get unpacked, but some lemonade and a cookie or two would taste good about now. Right?" She smiled at the younger woman and raised an eyebrow questioningly.

Hannah returned the smile. "Yes, they would. Thank you."

In a few minutes, she returned and sat near Elizabeth at the table. After a few swallows of lemonade and a bite of an oatmeal cookie, she declared, "This is very good, Mrs. Grissom. I appreciate your reviving me after a long trip."

"Well, I appreciate the opportunity to get acquainted. But, please, call me Elizabeth. We don't stand on formality too much around here. May I call you Hannah?"

"Please do. Everyone has been very friendly. Staying with Bea, when I came for the interview, was very pleasant. I try to think of Hunter as Mr. Grissom, since he's my boss, but Bea kept referring to him as Hunter. I think it stuck."

"That's fine with me, and I'm sure it'll be fine with him. Now, tell me about yourself, Hannah. Do you have family back in Kansas?"

A little shadow crossed Hannah's face, Elizabeth observed, but it quickly vanished.

"Yes, my parents and younger sister, Heidi. Dad is a manager at a loan company, and my mother is a home-maker. Heidi works as a law office receptionist."

"Well, we'll have to see that you don't miss them too much. We want you to enjoy your time here and our Montana hospitality."

"Oh, I'm sure I will. I'm excited about this teaching position and the opportunity to live in a different area of the country. Several members of the board talked of the isolation, but I look forward to the quiet evenings."

"That's good," Elizabeth chuckled, "because they are that. But, a person can find ways to fill them. Reading, knitting, television, hobbies, and such. Of course, you'll possibly have papers to grade and lessons to prepare."

"Yes, I certainly will." Hannah finished her second cookie. "I enjoy reading in my spare time, and I sometimes sew. I brought my portable machine with me. It may come in handy if the children want to do a holiday program for their parents."

Elizabeth agreed. "I'm handy with a sewing machine myself, though it's been years since I sewed a costume for my own children. Consider me a volunteer to help, if you need it, dear. I'd enjoy that."

"Why, thank you for the offer and for the refreshment. I should be going though." She briefly looked uncertain, then asked her hostess, "Is Hunter around? I'd like to get the keys and start unloading my car."

"He's somewhere out checking fence and cattle. I won't see him until suppertime. But I can give you the keys. Just a moment." She rose and went to another room. Back again, she said, "Here they are. I don't know which is which, but they fit the front doors. Just so you know, Hunter keeps a spare set in the ranch office, in case of emergency."

Surprised, Hannah only said, "Oh," then, "that's good to

know. I'll know where to come if I should lock myself out."

"Are you sure you don't want to wait for Hunter to come in? With having to park below the house, carrying boxes up the hill will be heavy work."

"Oh, I'm strong, and I don't want to impose on a busy man," she smiled. "Thanks again, Elizabeth. I'm happy to have met you."

They walked to the door, and Elizabeth stepped outside with her.

"Say, Hannah, please come back for supper. You don't have any food in the house, and I should have thought of that earlier. When Hunter comes in, I'll send him over. He can help you with the heaviest things, then bring you back to eat with us."

Hannah looked hesitant. "You're very generous, but . . . well, are you sure he won't mind? As I said, I don't want to impose on either of you."

"Nonsense, no imposition at all. I'll plan on your joining us for supper then." Hannah nodded. "Thanks again." She walked to her car and drove away.

Elizabeth stood on the steps and watched her car and the little cloud of dust it made until it was out of sight over the rise. She sighed and thought of her son. *She's a lovely young woman, not plain at all, Hunter.* But perhaps her son just hadn't looked at her with clear eyes. That old girlfriend had hurt him, and he seemed wary of getting entangled in a new relationship.

"More's the pity," she murmured, as she returned to her kitchen and cleared away the soiled glasses. She put the uneaten cookies back into a ceramic red apple cookie jar and turned to cooking. She had a beef roast with carrots and potatoes already in a slow cooker, and there was still pie for dessert. She'd serve warm apple sauce alongside. Hunter liked that.

She chuckled. She'd feed him comfort foods, since she had invited Hannah without his knowledge. Some of his favorite foods should soothe any ruffled feathers.

Then, feeling inspired, she put together a tuna-noodle casserole for Hannah to eat over the next few days. Elizabeth stood looking out the kitchen window and thought of the new addition to their small community. *I like that young woman. I sensed a certain tension when she spoke of her relatives. Could they be the reason she came to Whetstone? If so, it's our gain.*

Chapter Three

A few miles back to the west, Hannah reached the crossroads. This time she turned to her left and soon approached tiny Whetstone. She slowed, then pulled in at the gas pumps in front of the store. She thought it a good opportunity to fill up her tank after her trip.

Using a self-service pump, she went inside to pay. The door closed behind her with a jingle of its bell. She glanced around at the bright and pleasant room.

On her right, behind a half wall topped by pots of live greenery, was a small restaurant. It consisted of eight or so square tables covered by denim-blue cotton cloths. A small tin lantern holding a squat, white candle stood in the center of each. The flooring was of white and gray tile, and at the three windows hung blue and white checked curtains.

On her left was the general store. Hannah was pleased to see that it held more than she would have imagined from Bea's words. She had just decided to purchase some items for the next few days, when a middle-aged woman in casual shirt and jeans, her dark hair in a single braid down her back, entered from a door marked private at the rear of the room.

"Hello," she said pleasantly. "May I help you?"

"Hello. I just pumped some gas and also need some groceries." Hannah extended her hand, which the lady took in hers. "I'm the new schoolteacher, Hannah Morgan."

"Oh, yes. Welcome to Whetstone, Ms. Morgan. I'm Mary Jerome, and my husband, Jim, and I run this place. Take your time looking around, and I'll check you out whenever you're ready."

"Thanks, this is a nice business you have here. Larger than it appears from the outside."

"Thank you, we're proud of it ourselves," she responded with a wide smile.

Hannah chose milk, eggs, margarine, orange juice, bread, and cereal to go with the box of canned goods she'd brought from Kansas. Looking into a refrigerated case displaying cheeses and cold meats in bulk, she selected some Colby cheese and roast beef. Mrs. Jerome sliced and wrapped it in white glazed paper, tying each bundle with string.

"How very fresh that food looks," Hannah complimented. "I haven't seen cheese and meat sold in bulk for years, not since I visited my grandparents' farm in Kansas."

"Not quite the same as a city supermarket, is it?" Mary Jerome said with a smile. "But, it works well for us and our customers."

They moved to the cash register at the front of the store, and Hannah unloaded her basket, then paid. Seeing a rack of newspapers, she added a copy of the twice-weekly *Turk Talisman*.

"Perhaps, I'll learn what's happening in the area."

"Well, everyone's looking forward to meeting you, Ms. Morgan. The school board members spoke highly of you. Now our two sons are grown, so we don't have anyone in school, but I sure wish you well."

"Thanks. I appreciate that, and call me Hannah."

"I'd be pleased to and I'm Mary to anyone who comes in. I hope to see you again, real soon."

"I'm sure you will, Mary. Bye, now."

"Good-bye."

Hannah tucked her bags into the small space left on the floor of the passenger side and started the engine. Mary's quite a pleasant woman, she thought to herself. Now, if everyone I meet is as friendly, I'll be really lucky.

In no time at all, she had pulled into the schoolyard. She turned and backed her car up to the beginning of the path that led to the house. She began unloading by first carrying in her perishable groceries and storing them in the refrigerator. Looking around again at her new home, she was pleased to see that it looked freshly dusted and swept. "How thoughtful," she murmured as she went back to her car for another load.

Two hours later, she had put away her clothing in the closet and drawers of the loft bedroom. Hannah especially liked that feature of the little house. She had also made up the bed with the linens, pillows, blanket, and spread she had brought with her. Not knowing when she'd get to bed that night, she wanted it to be ready for her to fall into at a moment's notice. Next, she stocked the bathroom with her toiletries and towels.

She stepped off the porch to go for another load but paused when she saw a truck turning into the drive. Hannah recognized the white pickup with the Big G Cattle Company logo on its door as the one she'd seen at the ranch. Knowing it had to be Hunter, she hurried down the path to meet him. He got out and walked toward her.

"Hello, Mr. Grissom. It's good to see you again." She offered her hand which he shook briefly.

"Good afternoon, Ms. Morgan. I hope your trip was uneventful."

"It was, if you mean I had no trouble," she answered with a laugh. "No flat tires or speeding tickets or any other mishaps."

"That's good," he replied with a slight smile. "My

mother reported that you'd gotten in and stopped by for the keys. I hope you had no trouble finding the ranch?"

"Oh, no. Bea—I mean Mrs. Davidson—gave me perfect directions in the note she sent. But I must admit that it seemed I drove for miles before I found the buildings."

Hunter actually chuckled at that.

"It's only a bit more that a half mile, Ms. Morgan, but I suppose the first time a person drives in, it could seem longer." He sobered and asked, "Where do you want me to start? I understand I was volunteered to tote your heavy boxes."

"Yes, your mother insisted that I accept your help. I hope I'm not imposing on your time?"

"No, I came in earlier than usual today. Then, I'm to bring you home for supper."

Hannah wasn't sure if he really approved of that, but she smiled.

"Your mother's a very kind lady."

"That she is, Ms. Morgan." With those words, he hoisted the nearest box of books. "House or school?"

"House."

Within an hour, they had unloaded all the boxes, some of which went directly to the schoolroom. The majority Hannah wanted to sort through in the house first, so they were set in the living room.

She told Hunter what a surprise it had been to discover the small extra room beyond the bath on the ground floor. She hadn't noticed it the night Bea had shown her around.

"I can use it as an office or just as a storage room."

"When the house was built, they planned ahead. Just in case one of our teachers had a family and would need a second bedroom."

"Has anyone? Had a family, that is?" she asked, her head tilted to one side, quizzically.

Hunter looked at her. For some reason—he wasn't sure why—he liked that little motion.

"Uh, yes, a few over the years. Mrs. Tyler was married with a little boy. She taught and her husband minded the child and worked on a novel. It seemed to be an ideal situation for them."

"How long did they stay?" Hannah asked, while her mind processed that bit of information. She hoped whatever muse Mr. Tyler had found would still be present to inspire her own writing.

"For two years. Unfortunately, most stay only a year."

"That *is* unfortunate for the continuity of the pupils' learning."

"Yes, it seems we, the board, have to go through the hiring process every year." He frowned and leaned back against the kitchen counter, his legs crossed at the ankles and his arms folded across his broad chest. "Perhaps I shouldn't say this, Ms. Morgan, but that was the one objection I had to hiring you. I wasn't convinced that you would be able to handle the winter weather and the isolation. You're young and surely used to having more people around you, and there's not much to do around here."

Hannah smiled slowly. "I'm sure that the children are going to be enough people around me each day. The evenings will take care of themselves with lesson plans and grading papers. I read a lot, and I keep a journal. I like some television, and I brought several favorite old movies. I feel the days will pass quickly, perhaps too quickly."

"You sound sure."

"I am. While I'm looking forward to meeting parents and the people of Whetstone, I'm also looking forward to some personal time. Some time for introspection, if you will, away from my old, more hectic life in Topeka."

That made Hunter wonder if she were running away from something or *somebody*, but he kept his thoughts to himself.

"The weather won't be a problem, either. Believe me, we're used to blizzards in Kansas. I've even been snowed in on my grandparents' farm a few times," she added, hoping she was convincing him.

"Well, I hope things work out. May I even hope that you'll like us enough to stay a second year?" he suggested and grinned at her.

She smiled happily, her soft gray eyes sparkling. Hunter noted that she didn't seem plain when she did that. She had a lovely smile.

"Time will tell, Mr. Grissom. Would I be permitted to call you Hunter? Technically, you're my employer, but when Bea and your mother call you Hunter, it's difficult to not do the same."

"All right then, Hannah. We're not formal in these parts, as a rule."

"Of course, in public or at a board meeting, I'll use Mr. Grissom," she responded.

"I'll remember to call you Ms. Morgan too."

"Well, if you don't mind, I'll freshen up and change my shirt. I feel a little grimy from the boxes and the hours on the road."

"Go right ahead, Hannah." He glanced at his wristwatch. "Don't hurry. My mother's not expecting us until seven or so."

"I won't be long." She walked toward the bathroom, but Hunter stopped her with a word.

"I'll check to see that I locked the schoolhouse door behind me then wait on the porch." He picked up her set of keys that she'd left on the table and his hat from the couch.

"Fine," she replied. He must think he shouldn't be in here, while I'm changing clothes. He was truly a gentleman, Hannah surmised, as she closed the bathroom door behind her.

Fifteen minutes later, she stepped out onto the porch. Hunter was sitting on the top step, dangling his hat between his knees. He rose when he heard her and jammed his hat onto his head. He handed her the set of keys.

Hannah had changed into a green paisley blouse tucked into dark green pants. She had brushed out her pony tail, and her hair fell curving to her shoulders. She'd pulled some of it into a copper barette at the top of her head. The sunlight picked up a reddish glint in her brown hair and Hunter wondered why he had thought it was mousy brown.

Then, Hunter quickly quelled any thoughts about her looks. He was there to be polite and to help her out. Being Board Chairman sometimes went beyond simply conducting meetings.

"Before you lock the house, let me show you something." He pushed the door open, and she followed him inside. "This row of switches is set up to cover several outside lights as well as the living room's. Porchlight, security light in the parking area, front door of the school, and this last one will turn on a light inside the school."

"My goodness!" Hannah exclaimed. "How handy, and how very thoughtful. This'll make me feel much safer if I go down to the school after dark or on an early winter morning."

"And don't be concerned about the electricity, in fact leave the security light on all night, if you want."

"Thank you, Hunter. I have a feeling that you're the one who set this up too."

"Years ago. You aren't the first single woman to teach and live here." He didn't want her to think it was done recently, or especially for her.

"Of course," she replied, then wondered: *Why does he seem to run hot and cold? One moment, a little friendly, then quickly impersonal again? Oh, well, it doesn't matter. I'm not here looking for romance, for heaven's sake. I want a productive school year and a little tranquillity for myself.*

Thinking ahead, she flipped on both the porchlight and security light.

"For when I come back tonight," she murmured, then locked the door and let the screen door close behind them.

She led the way down the path, and they got into their vehicles. Hannah followed the truck out of the schoolyard and down the drive.

A short time later, she had greeted her hostess, and the three of them sat down to a delicious-looking meal.

"Thanks so much for inviting me, Elizabeth. I didn't think I was hungry, but this looks wonderful."

Hannah looked at the pretty red print cloth on the table. White dishes, sparkling glasses and utensils surrounded a small bouquet of colorful zinnias.

"I'm happy to have you here, Hannah. This is what I'd already planned for supper, so don't feel I went to any bother."

She glanced at her son across the table. He lowered his head, cleared his throat, and asked a blessing on their food, their guest, the upcoming school year, the welfare of the ranch, ranch hands, and the livestock.

"Amen," Hannah murmured with him and her hostess. She wondered about his expressed concern for the cattle.

"Yes, Hannah, this is one of my favorite meals, and Mom makes it often." He smiled casually and offered her first choice from the platter of sliced roast beef.

She pierced a slice, then took potatoes and carrots from a serving dish. She passed it to Hunter. Elizabeth slid a bowl of applesauce toward her.

Hannah was surprised that it was warm. "I've never eaten heated applesauce. It must be good that way."

"I never had either," Elizabeth said with a chuckle, "before I married into the Grissom Family. Tom, Hunter's father, enjoyed it that way, as does Hunter."

"It's the best. Homemade and warm. In fact, this is our own beef, carrots, and potatoes too."

"That's interesting, the whole meal's from your own resources. My grandparents, on my mother's side, farmed near a small Kansas town. They were largely self-sufficient as well, though their main crop was wheat. I spent summers with them when I was younger, and I helped Grandma with her garden. We canned and froze a lot of vegetables and fruits over the years. But I never had warm applesauce," she concluded with a smile.

"You didn't know what a treat you were missing," Hunter added.

"Are your grandparents still living, Hannah?" her hostess asked.

Hannah sipped from her glass of iced tea, then said, "Grandpa Withers had a stroke and died about four years ago. Grandma moved to town into a little apartment soon after. Now my mother's older brother, Edgar, works the farm. I didn't get to know my father's parents well, as they died in an accident when I was small."

"I'm sorry," Elizabeth said in sympathy. "My Tom died ten years ago. That was a difficult time for us." She looked at Hunter.

Hannah saw the briefest shake of his head. She supposed that he didn't want his mother to go into it with her there.

"Hunter assumed the running of the ranch at that time, and he does a fine job of it." Elizabeth smiled proudly at him.

Hannah commented, "It must keep you very busy."

"Yes, but I like to keep busy."

"I find that to be true as well," Hannah said.

No one spoke for awhile, then Hannah remembered the house.

"It was very thoughtful of someone to come in and dust and sweep the teacher's house before I arrived."

"That was Olive and George Bergman, the school custodians. She wanted it to be spotless—her words—for your arrival," Hunter said.

"Well, I appreciated it. I'll thank her when I meet them."

"That may be on Sunday," Hunter suggested. "This is the Sunday for Pastor Blake to come out from Turk to preach. Knowing there'd be a good turnout, Bea and some of the other ladies thought it'd be an excellent time to introduce you to the community." He looked a bit uncertain. "I hope you don't mind our springing that on you."

"Oh, not at all. I'd planned to go to church anyway."

Elizabeth inserted, "Bea is our social organizer around Whetstone, and we enjoy her ideas and plans for the most part."

"Actually the plan involves a community-wide potluck dinner after church." Again Hunter looked at her. She felt he was gauging her response.

Hannah said brightly, "How nice. I'll enjoy that. It's a little more informal—more casual."

Elizabeth stood to serve dessert and coffee. When she placed a piece of apple pie before Hannah, the young woman looked up with a twinkle in her gray eyes.

"From your own orchard, Elizabeth?"

"Yes it is, the fruit anyway." She laughed and sat down again.

"I'll have to come up with something for the potluck," Hannah said quietly, almost to herself.

"Just being there will be enough, Hannah," Hunter said, graciously. "That reminds me. How are you fixed for food? I carried in a box of canned goods, but the little Whetstone Store has fresh milk, bread, and such."

Hannah smiled. "Bea very kindly told me about it when we drove by the night of the interview. In fact after I picked up the keys today, I gassed up the car and bought some things. I introduced myself to Mary Jerome. She was very friendly."

"She is, and I think you'll find that most everyone is," Elizabeth agreed.

"That's good to hear. I've found that a certain feature of your personality that one person *likes* may be the same thing that another person *dislikes*."

Hunter wondered if that had colored her decision to

move to Montana, but he didn't want to ask questions about it.

Instead, he commented, "All of us run into people like that, I'm afraid."

Hannah nodded in agreement, then, changing the subject, said, "I saw a beautiful gray horse in a corral when I pulled in tonight. What's his name?"

Hunter actually beamed. Talking horses was just his thing, and he replied, "That's The General. I've ridden him for about eight years now. Do you like to ride?"

"Yes . . . well, I used to. Not a horse like The General though. My grandparents had a white mare named Starlight. She was old and slow, just my speed when I was a girl. Grandma didn't worry when I took Starlight out across the fields. She knew that *no one* could make that mare break into a gallop." Hannah giggled and tossed her head at the happy memory.

Hunter just stared, a fact that didn't go unnoticed by his mother, observant woman that she was.

Elizabeth said, "I'm going to clear the table now. Hunter, take Hannah down to the horse barn and introduce her to The General and Ike. Oh, I'll send the last piece of pie with you for Ike."

Hunter took his eyes away from Hannah, cleared his throat, and agreed.

"Thank you for a lovely meal, but I should help you with the cleanup, Elizabeth," she protested.

"Not necessary, dear. I'll load the dishwasher and be done in a jiffy."

"Okay," Hannah replied, then looked for a sign from Hunter that they were going. He rose, so she did. Elizabeth handed her the wrapped pie. Hunter grabbed his hat, and they left the house.

They covered the five hundred feet to the barns in silence. Hannah was trying to think of something to say, when he opened a sliding wooden door on one of the buildings.

"This's the horse barn," he said and let her step in ahead of him. When Hannah's eyes adjusted to the dimmer light, she was surprised at the number of stalls. A wide aisle ran down the middle separating them into two rows. Hunter flipped a light switch, and she could see how clean and well-kept everything was. She breathed deeply of the mix of fresh straw, hay, and animal odors. It reminded her of the many happy hours she'd spent helping and playing in her grandfather's barn in Kansas. She smiled happily at the sudden memory.

A door opened to their left, and an older man asked, "That you, Hunter?" He stepped through, then stopped short when he saw Hannah.

"Hi, Ike. This is Hannah Morgan, the new schoolteacher. We had her over for supper, being that it's her first day in Whetstone. Hannah, this is Ike, Isaac Greene, the keeper of the horses and horse barn, and the man who *really* runs the ranch."

Hannah could tell that Hunter almost meant that literally, but Ike just guffawed at his words. "Pleased to meet you, young lady. Welcome, and I hope you like it here."

"Thank you, Ike." She shook his hand. "I think I will. Oh, Elizabeth sent this down for you." She smiled warmly and thrust the slice of pie into his hands.

His eyes lit up. "Thank her for me, please. No one makes pie like Elizabeth," he added admiringly.

"It's very good," Hannah agreed.

"Hannah likes horses, so I brought her down to meet The General. How is Cinnamon doing?"

"Better. That second shot the doc gave her has helped. She's been putting her weight on that leg these last few days."

"Good. See you, Ike," Hunter said. He took Hannah's

elbow and escorted her down the aisle to the last stall on the left.

Ike watched them walk away, a bemused smile on his lined face. Now there was a real nice gal, the old-timer thought, and pretty too. *I sure hope that boy notices.* He turned to the tackroom and the comfortable chair where he'd been enjoying an evening doze. He unwrapped the pie and enjoyed that too.

The General and three other horses had been brought in for the night. He looked up in anticipation as Hunter neared.

"Hello, old fellow. No, we're not going out for a ride tonight." Hannah smiled at the expression in the gray's eyes.

"I almost think he understood you. He looks disappointed." Hunter stroked The General's neck. "He's always up for a ride, aren't you, fellow?"

The horse nickered and nodded his head. Hannah laughed aloud at that, and The General moved closer to her.

"I think he likes your laugh. Go ahead and pet him." She did, stroking one hand along his neck. "You're lovely, aren't you, sweetheart? So pretty, or should I say handsome?"

She laughed, softly. Hunter smiled.

"He's sure eating up your attention."

"I'm curious, Hunter. Why did you name him The General?"

"His full name is General Lee, for his beautiful gray coat. Made me think of the real Robert E. Lee in his Rebel uniform."

"Oh, I like that," Hannah responded. "Are you a history buff, Hunter?"

"I suppose you could say that. It's one of my interests. Minored in history at college."

"Along with a major in . . . ?"

"Livestock and rangeland management. What else?" He smiled across the horse's head at her.

She swallowed hard at that smile. "Yes, what else, when you have a property to maintain? You know the details of my education from my application. Where did you go to college?"

"Again, where else? The university in Bozeman has a College of Agriculture. I'm a pure Montanan—born here, raised here, educated here. I expect I'll die here."

"In that respect, I guess I'm a pure Kansan. I've never lived anywhere else, until now. Have you ever wanted a change, Hunter?"

"Oh, in my rebellious youth maybe. No, not seriously. I love this land, and I always knew I'd be the one to take over after Dad. But I didn't think it would be so soon after I finished college."

Hunter knows where he came from and where he's going. How wonderful that must feel, to be so certain. Hannah sighed inwardly.

"Yes, it's obvious that your mother still misses your father." When he didn't say anything, she added, "It's nice that you have Ike around."

"He's been here from the beginning. He was Dad's foreman, and he's a big help to me. A wealth of good, practical information."

"I liked him," she murmured.

Hunter smiled. "He liked you too."

Hannah returned his smile and felt a bit embarrassed.

"Tell General Lee goodnight and come with me across the way. I want you to meet Strawberry and Cinnamon."

She said good-bye, then he led her to a stall on the opposite wall where a pretty strawberry roan stood dozing on her feet. Hunter spoke to her, and the horse came toward them.

"What a pretty girl you are! This has to be Strawberry with a coat like that."

"Yes, she has the classic strawberry roan shading. She belongs to my mother who's had her for a good many years. Mom jokes about two old ladies going out for a ride."

Hannah smiled. Hunter moved down the aisle to a stall nearer the tackroom, and she followed. There she was introduced to the most beautiful young mare she'd ever seen. Her coat was a lovely shade of cinnamon-brown, and she had a striking white blaze between her soulful brown eyes. The horse had been lying down but got to her feet and met them at the door in the front of her stall.

"Oh my, Hunter. She's gorgeous! I can see that she truly matches her name."

"It's the right foreleg that was bothering her. An inflammation in a joint. But she got up and moved more easily that time."

"Yes, she seemed to."

Hunter talked to the horse, stroked her neck, and urged Hannah to do the same. The mare responded to her, not appearing afraid of her at all.

Hunter had a sudden idea.

"Say, Hannah, would you like to come over and ride with me one day? Cinnamon's healing well, and she'll soon be able to take the weight of a rider again. You wouldn't be too heavy for her. Much better than one of the hands."

Hannah nearly whooped in excitement. "I'd love it! But, remember that I'm not a very good rider. Will Cinnamon welcome a greenhorn on her back?"

"She's very adaptable, aren't you, girl?" Hunter nuzzled his face against the mare's neck. "I think she'd be the perfect mount for you."

"Wonderful!"

They talked for a few more minutes while Hannah met

a sorrel named Gabby that belonged to Ike, then they strolled back to the house. Tired from her trip, Hannah bade them goodnight. After again thanking Elizabeth for her meal, she gratefully accepted the tuna casserole her hostess had made, then left to drive back to her new home.

Hunter stood in the yard and watched until her car crested the rise in the lane. He realized that he hadn't talked so much to a young woman in years, especially about himself. Amazing.

Chapter Four

Hannah kept busy over the next few days. She put her kitchen in order, tried out the washer and drier, and sorted through the boxes in the living room.

She spent time arranging her eclectic collection of books on the ample shelves on either side of the fireplace. A cupboard under the television stand held her videotapes, and she fit her radio, CD player and CDs on one of the bookshelves. She proudly set an antique clock and a pair of silver candlesticks on the mantel. Grandma Withers had given them to her when she moved away from the farm and Hannah treasured them dearly.

There was a small table and a chest of drawers in the spare room. She set her laptop on the table and her portable sewing machine in the closet. It was a good place to keep her coats, boots, and other cold weather gear conveniently downstairs.

On the afternoon of her second full day in the house, Bea Davidson called on her, bearing a basket of gifts.

"Just call me the unofficial welcoming committee lady!" she said with a hearty laugh. "I hope you like plants, but even if you don't like to fuss with them, this philodendron is nearly indestructible. Just let it have light and some water, and it'll flourish."

"Oh, lovely, Bea! Thank you. Yes, I do enjoy plants and flowers. In fact I was thinking of driving into Turk to buy a few plants and pots for both here and the classroom before school starts." Hannah set the plant in its blue ceramic pot on a table under the front window. "That should be a good spot for it. I thought it'd give me an excuse to look around the town too," she added with a smile.

"Good idea, dear. Now you'll want to put this gelatin salad into the refrigerator," she instructed as she lifted the container from her basket. "And here are a few fresh-baked cookies."

"Yum, chocolate chip! How did you know my favorite, Bea?" She laughed happily as she carried the Jell-O to the kitchen. Putting it away, she took out a pitcher of iced tea. "Let's have some tea and cookies, Bea. I'm ready for a break from unpacking."

Hannah cleared a space on the table, and they sat down with their glasses and cookies to share.

"Actually," Bea began, "I just remembered that Olive Bergman took several plants home with her after the school year ended last June. She thought she'd re-pot some that had grown rootbound and keep them over the summer. I expect she'll be bringing them back one of these days."

"I'll look forward to that. Meeting her and seeing the plants."

"Speaking of meeting people, there'll be a potluck meal after church service this Sunday. I hope you can come and be introduced, Hannah."

"Yes, I plan on it. Hunter mentioned it when I had supper with and him Elizabeth Tuesday evening. He thought I might mind, but I think it'll be a comfortable way to meet the children and their parents and others in the community."

"Yes, it should, and this is the Sunday for the preacher to be there too. There should be a good many people on hand. Now don't bother bringing a dish, as it's your first time. Just table service for yourself."

"Thank you. Hunter said much the same thing."

"I'm glad that you met Elizabeth already. She's a fine woman."

"I enjoyed meeting her when I stopped for the keys. Hunter was out and about the ranch somewhere, she said, so she found them for me. Then a couple hours later, he showed up to help me unload the heavier things, and I followed him back to the ranch at Elizabeth's request."

Bea smiled. "Hunter's a good man. Works hard to keep that ranch thriving. Active in the community too, but he still manages to keep to himself. Not much for the ladies, though there are some around here who'd like to change that." She gave a nod of her white curls.

"Oh, I'm sure there are," Hannah agreed with a chuckle. "He's nice-looking and owns a handsome piece of property. That's enough to have the ladies buzzing around."

"Elizabeth thought he was going to get married about five years back, but it fell through. He doesn't talk about it. And, *I* shouldn't be talking about our Board Chairman's love life or lack thereof," Bea concluded with an ornery little grin.

"Well, just to set the record straight, Bea, I'm not interested in romance while I'm here. I just want to do my best for my pupils, enjoy some quiet time and explore the area a little."

"Oh, that's almost a shame, Hannah, but whatever pleases you, dear. Now, I'll be going so you can get back to your unpacking and arranging."

They both rose, and Hannah carried their glasses and cookie plate to the kitchen counter.

"Yes, I'm afraid I've a lot of that to do yet. But I'm glad you stopped by, and thanks again for the gifts, Bea. You're very thoughtful."

"You're welcome, Hannah." As she stepped out onto the porch, she added, "See you on Sunday."

"Yes, bye now."

Hannah watched Bea's mini-van out to the road, then got her keys. Picking up a box of books, she walked down to the schoolhouse and unlocked the door. She made enough trips to transfer the rest of the books and other classroom things she had brought.

Standing inside the door, she looked around. Her first impression had been a good one, and she realized that it held up after ten or twelve days.

Smiling to herself, she began taking inventory of the available supplies, added hers to it, and listed some items she might buy for the classroom on her trip to Turk.

Next, she found an unused four-shelf cheaply-made bookcase in the garage and moved it near the other library corner shelves. It was large enough to hold the additional books she'd brought to enlarge the library selection. She dusted it, and filled it with the books.

Hannah finally took a break and sat down at her desk. On it was a new monthly calendar deskpad and a teacher's planner. To one side was a box of new textbooks that some-one had brought in since the night of her interview. Hannah eagerly delved into the box, and set out the new readers and American history books. In a second box were work-books for geography, spelling, writing, and English. She put the hardback books on shelves near other texts and stacked the workbooks above them. Then she gathered the teacher's guides and sample texts and workbooks together to take to her house. She could sit more comfortably while she read and made lesson plans to cover the first few weeks and overall plans for the year. Hannah believed in prepa-ration.

Still at her new desk, Hannah looked over the list of pupils' names and grade levels then looked out over the array of desks. It seemed strange to her to see three or four different sizes. Previously, of course, she'd taught at one grade level with similarly-sized seats. She made a mental note of how she might arrange them, but it was getting late. She put her planning materials in an empty box, turned off the lights, and locked the door behind her.

Back at her house, she washed her hands and face. Feeling hungry, once she noted that it was past seven o'clock, she made a sandwich from the cheese and sliced beef she'd purchased from Mary Jerome. She carried it, a glass of milk, and a small dish of Bea's gelatin salad to the living room and set her supper on an endtable. She organized the textbooks, guides, and workbooks in the order she planned to peruse them.

Hannah began with the primary readers and related subjects for that age level. She had progressed to the third level when the phone rang. She jumped, as it hadn't rung since she'd moved into the house.

Laughing at herself, she rose and walked to the wall phone in the kitchen. "Hello."

"Hello, Hannah."

It was Hunter, which greatly surprised Hannah. It hadn't occured to her that he might call.

"Hi, Hunter." She waited for him to respond.

"Just calling to see that everything's okay. No problems with the house or the school building?"

"Uh, no . . . none at all. I've got the house more or less in order, and I began work on the classroom this afternoon. Lots to do yet, but it'll get done. I'm spending this evening getting familiar with the guides and textbooks."

"Then you found the boxes on your desk?"

"Yes, I did. Wonderful to have brand new readers and history books to use. I've found that students can get excited about being the first to use a book."

There was a pause. Then, "Yeah, I kind of remember that feeling when I was a kid."

Hannah giggled. "I do too. I love the smell of a new book. Sounds silly, doesn't it?"

He chuckled, and Hannah's smile grew broader.

"No, not silly. Before I forget, I think Cinnamon will be ready to ride come Sunday. Ike's given his okay too. So after the potluck and socializing, would you like to drive over here? We'll take her and The General out for awhile."

Hannah was elated. "Oh, that'll be great, Hunter! I'll look forward to it." Her mind raced through her wardrobe. "Say, can a girl in sneakers legally ride a horse around here? Not exactly western-wear, I know."

"Sure you can. Cinnamon won't mind a bit."

"Good. One of these days, I'll have to shop for cowgirl boots and a proper western hat," she replied, her voice bubbling.

"I hope you do," Hunter commented. "Maybe if you invest in boots and a hat, you'll decide to stay as our teacher for more than just one year."

"Who knows, maybe I will."

"Oh, the other reason I called is that the piano tuner will be out tomorrow morning about nine. His name's Jessup. I hope you can be there to let him into the school? I apologize for not letting you know earlier, but he's really busy this time of year. We were lucky he fit us into his schedule, since he has to drive out from Bozeman."

"Of course, I'll be here, and thanks for making the arrangements. Is he the person who's tuned it in other years?"

Hannah sat on a stool that was near the wall phone. The call was lasting longer than she would have imagined. Not that she minded. Talking to *this* Board Chairman was interesting. Quite different from conversations with pompous Mr. J. W. Briggs of her former school district.

"Yes, he's done it regularly for years. Well, I should let you go back to your books, and I have some work on the computer to finish yet tonight."

"Goodnight then, Hunter. Thanks for calling and for the invitation to ride on Sunday."

"You're welcome. 'Night, Hannah."

As she hung up the receiver, she wondered at the warmth in his voice. Soft, melting, chocolate came to mind. Shaking her head dismissively, she returned to her living room and books.

Becoming engrossed in the books, Hannah stayed up later than she'd planned, but she was awake, dressed and waiting for the piano tuner well before nine the next morning.

She let Mr. Jessup into the school and returned to her planning. Sometime later, he came up to the house to say that he was finished. Hannah thanked him, and the man left.

She had made good progress with her work. She decided to reward herself with a trip into Turk. She gathered her shoulderbag and the supply list she'd begun earlier and locked both the house and school doors, then drove away.

Hannah enjoyed the drive into Turk, and she spent time exploring it a bit by car before she shopped. It was larger than it had seemed from her earlier quick trips through back and forth to Gallatin Field, the Bozeman area airport.

She intentionally located the high school, middle, and elementary schools, as she would be required to attend a series of meetings there the next week before the first day of school.

Hannah parked on Madison Street near a bookstore and office supply combination and went inside. Consulting her list, she was pleased to be able to find the items she wanted for the classroom. Keeping to the budget the board had given her, she selected some additional paints, markers, colored paper, and a few other things to supplement the supplies already at the school. She purchased a colorful variety of crepe paper rolls, as she liked to use it as edging on bulletin boards.

Hannah placed her bags to one side of the counter, then looked through the books available in the bookstore side of the shop. She didn't purchase any, but made note of a few possibilities, if she couldn't find them at a better price from a catalogue.

A few minutes later, she stored her bags in the car. Deciding to stroll both sides of the main street, she set out. Passing one of the restaurants, Hannah couldn't resist checking out a place named The Cowboy Cafe. Thinking that she really was in cowboy country, she went inside.

Two walls were lined with booths, and several tables filled the center of the eating area. Hannah slid into a booth and looked around at the western decor. She grinned, but admitted to herself that she liked its rustic look.

Home cooking was offered on the menu, and she chose a bowl of hearty potato-cheese soup, a small green salad, and iced tea. Hannah enjoyed her lunch thoroughly. When she paid for her meal, she noticed a rack of postcards near the cash register and selected a few for family and friends back in Kansas.

Meaning to shop for additional groceries while in Turk, she first walked down the street to the post office for stamps.

Hannah then crossed the street to go to her car. She stopped at Jackson's Western Wear to admire the clothing, hats, and boots in the window. There was a sale going on, but she still hesitated. Moving had added a good bit to her credit card balance but buying something distinctly western appealed to her.

She went inside and came out a half an hour later with a beige cowgirl hat that sported a red feather tucked into its brown hatband.

She grinned, very pleased with her purchase. The boots she'd tried on had been tempting, but they could wait.

She'd loved the shirt and ruffles-on-the-bottom skirt she'd tried, too. But, since she was going riding on Sunday, the hat seemed just the thing to wear with her jeans.

She made buying groceries her last stop, then drove home. While she'd found most of the items on her list, she planned to explore Bozeman in the near future.

Hannah spent Saturday arranging desks, decorating the classroom, and seeing that all was ready for her students' first day.

Her labor was pleasantly interrupted by a phone call from Olive Bergman. The wall phone near the kitchenette was a convenient extension of the house phone, Hannah learned. A few minutes later, George and Olive drove in and greeted Hannah warmly. She helped them carry in the school's plants and arranged them on windowsills and tabletops. A small bronze chrysanthemum made a bright spot on the corner of her desk.

Olive chatted with Hannah, while George insisted that he give the floor one last dustmopping before he left. Hannah liked the congenial couple. They gave her a few pointers on which windows may stick if opened too wide, how to start a fire in the heating stove if necessary, and other gems of wisdom she found useful. Their number was written on a list beside the phone for emergencies too, George mentioned with a smile.

Hannah thanked them and saw them to their car. She felt fortunate to have met another friendly, welcoming couple. She then returned to her work.

Sunday morning found Hannah making the short drive into Whetstone. The church's parking lot was nearly full, but she found a place at the end of a row. She was surprised to find Hunter Grissom lounging against a railing on the front steps.

Hannah took in his appearance in one quick look as she

approached. He was in a gray western-cut suit, white shirt
with a black bolo tie, and a white hat. She even noticed his
highly-polished black boots. Wow! So this is how a rancher
dressed up for Sunday looks, she thought. No wonder he
turns the ladies' heads!

"Good morning, Hunter," she said quietly and paused at
the foot of the steps.

Hunter had watched her walk toward him since she
stepped out of her car. Despite the rough gravel under the
flimsy white sandals on her feet, she moved gracefully. She
wore her hair up as at the interview. Some instinct told him
that she did that to appear older. Why, he couldn't fathom.
Her dress was yellow with white embroidery around the
neckline and down the front. She looked cool, pretty, and
like spring sunshine to him. For some reason, that thought
seemed to make his heart swell in his chest, until he suddenly swallowed hard.

"Morning, Hannah." His voice was a bit gruff, and she
looked sharply at him. But he offered his hand as she began
to climb the steps. "Mother went on inside, but I thought
I'd wait for you. Will you sit with us for your first time
here?"

"Why, thank you. That'd be very nice."

They paused in the vestibule and accepted the church
bulletins a greeter handed them. Hannah murmured, "Good
morning," in response to the gentleman's greeting.

Inside she found the sanctuary to be typical of a simple
country church built at least a hundred years earlier, she
surmised. As Bea had predicted, the wooden pews were
nearly full. Hannah returned the smiles of greeting as Hunter led her to a seat on the right.

"Good morning, Hannah," Elizabeth said warmly, as she
slid over to make room for her and Hunter, who sat at the
end of the pew.

"Good morning. It feels a little strange knowing that

everyone knows who I am, but I don't know them," she whispered.

Elizabeth smiled and returned her whisper. "Now that'll change soon enough. Hunter plans to introduce you at the end of the service, then it's up to the others to introduce themselves at the potluck dinner."

Hannah enjoyed the worship service. The pastor gave a meaningful sermon, there was a small choir, and she had always liked singing hymns herself. Through it all, she tried not to let her nerves build. She needed to present a friendly, but cool and competent facade to the local people. She wasn't at her best in crowds.

Near the end of the service, the pastor nodded to Hunter. He rose and stepped out into the aisle. Clearing his throat, he greeted the congregation.

"Good morning, all. As you know, the board has hired a new teacher. I'd like you to meet Ms. Hannah Morgan, most recently of Topeka, Kansas, now of Whetstone, Montana." He looked at her with a smile, and she stood at the end of the pew. She glanced around the sanctuary and gave her best smile. Her cheeks grew pink when the gathering applauded her in welcome. "The board hopes you'll be able to stay for the potluck and take the opportunity to introduce yourself to Ms. Morgan."

Hannah added a thank you for the warm welcome. She sat down with a small sigh of relief. Hunter sat also. Then they stood again for the final hymn and the benediction.

Filing out of the church, she remembered her table service she'd left in the car. Hunter took her keys and was soon back with her basket, then he escorted her to the basement of the church. There was a kitchen to one side and tables and chairs had been set up in an open area.

Most of the congregation had stayed, if the crowd was any indication. Bea and Hunter stood with her in an informal receiving line where she met her pupils, their parents, and many other members of the community.

She was pleased to meet the wives of the board members. Bea's husband, Fred, was there too. Mary Jerome introduced her husband, Jim. Hannah had noticed a chairlift on the basement stairs. She assumed there was a concrete ramp at ground level somewhere to avoid the entrance steps.

Finally, the line ended as people moved on to the tables of food. Hannah felt a bit drained and welcomed Hunter's complaint that he was starved. "Let's eat!"

In a few minutes, the three of them had filled their plates and joined Elizabeth and Bea's husband at a table.

"This really looks good," Hannah commented and took a bite of potato salad.

"I'm so hungry, anything would look good," Hunter added with a grin.

"Yeah, Hunter, I'm not sure how you managed to stay put in that line with everyone else filling their plates," teased Fred Davidson with a hearty chuckle.

Bea and Elizabeth laughed as well. Hannah wasn't sure if she should join in the laughter.

"I think it's called self-control, Fred," Hunter replied. He smiled warmly at the others. "But I was nearing its end."

"I appreciated Bea's and your standing with me, Hunter. It . . . it made it easier." She nodded her thanks to Bea as well.

"Oh, you're welcome, dear," that lady responded.

"No problem," Hunter said quietly, as he looked up and met her gaze across the table. She looked so somber, he smiled to reassure her. He was rewarded by a sweet smile in return. Both quickly dropped their eyes to their plates.

The conversation at their table drifted around them for a few minutes while they ate. Then Fred asked, "Hunter, how's it going with your summer pasture?" He was referring to the leased land in the foothills of the mountain range to the east of the Big G Cattle Company Ranch.

Hunter used his paper napkin and sat back.

"No problems so far, Fred. We're lucky to have an allotment that's pretty well-watered and so the grass is in better shape. I figure I'll have to buy hay this winter though, since I got only two cuttings off that field to the south."

Hannah's ears perked up. She was interested in knowing what happened to the ranchers. Her students came from ranching families.

"I figure the same on the Ruby. I've even thought of buying extra hay early. Maybe I could beat the price later on when everyone may need it."

"That's a sound idea. Buy now, before the demand and price goes sky-high," Hunter agreed. "Do you think we'd get an even better deal if we went in together on a couple of loads?"

"Most likely. I'll check the market tomorrow. The fire danger makes me nervous too. If I have to bring my herd in early, the pasture on the Ruby won't hold them for very long. This's been a terribly hot, dry summer." He shook his head to emphasize his words.

"Yes," Elizabeth agreed, "it surely has been. The worst since eighty-eight, I'd say."

"Or ninety-five," Bea inserted. "We've been lucky that the wildfires have been in other areas this year. I pray that it stays that way."

"Amen," added her husband. "Say, Hunter, I was talking to Chuck Carson a bit ago. He and his crew were checking on his herd last week. He suspects he's lost about thirty. Now he's not sure it's rustlers as some may just be off in some of those coulees on that allotment of his, but who knows?"

"Rustlers?" Hannah asked in an awed whisper. "I mean, I didn't think rustlers still existed." She looked embarrassed at her outburst. "I'm sorry, I didn't mean to interrupt."

"That's okay, Hannah," Hunter assured her. "But yes, we do still have an outbreak of that every few years. Mostly when cattle prices are good, and the thieves can get more for them."

"My goodness, I'm surprised."

"It's so, Ms. Morgan. The Ruby Ranch was hit last spring in broad daylight, we think. Roy Pringle lost a good number about a year ago."

"And now, maybe Carson's place," Hunter added, disgustedly. "So far, we seem to be okay. Pike hired a couple extra hands to go with the boys to watch the herd closer this summer. Cookie's set up a cook camp to keep them well-fed and happy. Mom, Ike and I are the only ones on the ranch most days, though the guys trade off coming in for a rest every so often. It's costing us, but I hope it keeps us from losing any cattle."

"We hope so too," Bea commented.

"Sounds like a good plan, Hunter," Fred added.

Elizabeth inserted, "I've been cooking for the hands when they come down from the hills. I'm rather enjoying it. Seems like old times. Of course, the guys like to head into Turk or Bozeman for part of their time off."

"No doubt," Fred said and chuckled. "Well, Mother, if you're ready, shall we head home?"

"Of course, dear. This has been enjoyable. The best of luck with the school year, Hannah, and we'll see you all soon." Bea got up and gathered their tableware and went to look for her empty food dish. Fred said good-bye and followed her.

"Well, I'll get my dishes too." Elizabeth took Hunter's from him and put them with hers into a picnic basket and headed for the kitchen.

Many of the people had started to leave. A few of the children came over to tell the new teacher good-bye. Among them was the set of blond, blue-eyed, twin girls that would make up her first grade class: Nancy and Darcy Gunderson.

"Bye, girls. I'll be seeing you in a few days," Hannah

told them warmly. The twins beamed at her and went to join their mother.

"Looks like you've won them over already," Hunter said with a grin.

"Well, little girls often like going to school, you know. More so than some little boys."

Hunter laughed. "That's probably true! I remember days when I would have much rather been fishing. But then, I can't remember having a teacher quite like you."

Hannah's eyebrows rose in surprise. Then she quickly ducked her head to reach under the table for her basket. Her mind raced. *That sounds like a compliment! Just ignore it.* When she came up with her basket, she put her soiled tableware in it. She tried to look composed.

"Is the plan to go riding this afternoon still good? I told Cinnamon and The General you were coming over. Don't want to disappoint them." His words and grin disarmed her.

"Of course. I'll go home, change, and be over in an hour. Okay?"

"Okay." He stood and found his hat and his mother. He took the picnic basket from her, and they left.

Hannah followed soon after. Saying good-bye and thanking people for the nice dinner and pleasant time, as she moved slowly toward the door, took longer than she would have thought.

Chapter Five

Hannah was only a few minutes late. Hunter must have heard her car. He hailed her from the horse barn door.

"Down here, Hannah."

"I'll just return your mother's casserole dish first," she shouted back with a wave.

She walked up to the porch door and rapped on it. Elizabeth answered from the kitchen, "Coming."

Hannah gave her the clean dish and thanked her again for her generosity, then turned to go to the barn.

"Have fun, dear. Cinnamon is a joy to ride."

"Thank you, Elizabeth. See you later."

She watched the young woman walk toward the horse barn thinking: *I wonder if Hunter is taking Bea's suggestion that he entertain our new teacher to heart or is he just a little interested in her. I wish I knew, but that son of mine can keep his thoughts very much to himself, when he wants. Well, I can hope, anyway.*

She closed the door and returned to her kitchen. She decided to bake a cake—a nice, rich chocolate cake. If Hannah can't stay for a piece, she'd have it on hand for Hunter and any of the cowboys who came in for a break this week.

In the barn, Hunter had just saddled The General when Hannah stepped inside. He stopped and watched her walk toward him, something that he seemed to like doing these days.

She wore sneakers, a white T-shirt under a long-sleeved red cotton shirt, both tucked into well-worn jeans. On her head was a tan cowgirl hat with a red feather in the hatband. Brand-new, if he wasn't mistaken.

He grinned a welcome. "Like your new hat."

She laughed. "Thank you. I went to Turk Friday afternoon and looked around. I resisted the boots and a lovely ruffled skirt but not this hat." She touched its brim in a salute.

"You'll need it too. The sun will be hot again this afternoon."

They'd slowly walked to Cinnamon's stall. He'd hung a saddle over the divider. It was an older one that his mother had once used, and he thought it would fit Hannah nicely.

After a few words to the beautiful animal and a pat or two, Hannah asked, "May I try to saddle her myself, Hunter? It's been a few years. In fact I often rode Starlight bareback, but I hope I can still do it."

"Go right ahead."

He watched as she smoothed the saddle blanket over Cinnamon's back, talking all the while to her in a soothing voice. Then she hoisted the saddle off the divider and, with one test lift, onto the horse's back.

"There," she exclaimed triumphantly. "I think I just used a few muscles that I haven't used for years. Thank you, Cinnamon, for standing so still for me." She patted the horse's neck then turned to fastening the girth.

"She's good about saddles. Doesn't haul in air to fool you into leaving it loose. But I'll check it for you this first time, if you'd like?"

"Yes, please do."

Hunter ran his hands around the girth and decided it was

tight enough but not too tight. He checked the rest of the rigging as well.

Hannah then slipped the bridle over Cinnamon's head. Hunter adjusted the bit, then handed Hannah the reins. "A fine job, Hannah. Let's take them outside." He opened the stall door.

Feeling proud that she had done well, Hannah led Cinnamon out of the stall, down the aisle, and through the open door. They waited, Hannah talking sweet-talk to the mare, until Hunter and The General joined them.

Gathering the reins in her left hand, Hannah mounted a little awkwardly but successfully. Hunter asked if the length of the stirrups was too short or long, but she thought they felt just right.

He swung easily into his saddle, and they were off. Cinnamon fell into a walk to The General's left just a little to the back of his large head. They crossed a dusty open area between barns, which Hunter said were the hay barn and the cattle barn. Off to the left in the shade of a large cottonwood tree was the bunkhouse for the hands.

"Why are the buildings so far apart?"

"Mainly in case of fire. This way we'd have a better chance of saving the others if one caught on fire." By this time, they were passing a small earthen dam holding back a pond. "That's why they and the house have metal roofs too. My father put in this pond both for the cattle and for a source of water to fight a fire."

"I hope you've never had to use it for that."

"No, we've been lucky. Used it for swimming too." He grinned over at her. "We had some good times there."

"That sounds nice."

Hunter said, "It was." Then, "Let's try a trot, Hannah. Are you game?"

"Okay!"

It went well, considering how long it had been for Hannah. But she knew she bounced a little too much in the saddle. They had been climbing steadily. Now Hunter slowed and she followed his lead. The horses picked their way down off a ridge and headed straight for water.

Their riders reined in and dismounted. The horses drank from a stream.

"This spring up here," he pointed then walked to it, "is the source for the stream we've seen off and on on our ride up, and it's the one that was dammed to create the pond. The overflow from the pond ambles through the pastures, then joins Clear Creek a few hundred yards upstream from the school property."

"So is all the land around the school part of your ranch? The creek too?"

"Uh-huh. The creek's accessible to the public for fishing, as long as they stay close to the banks and don't litter."

"Well, may I have your permission to use it, sort of as an outdoor lab? When I was looking through the fifth grade science book, it came to me that there was a lab on our doorstep. I thought we'd make a study of the creek, the plants and grasses, the fish, birds, and small animals we might find, and contrast it during its different seasons. I was walking around the schoolgrounds yesterday and found the oddest thing, an old-fashioned, wooden stile built over the back fence next to a corner post."

Hunter laughed.

"You knew it was there, didn't you?" she asked, smiling at his laughter.

"Yeah, my dad and I built it more than twenty years ago. I never liked to take the bus, so I'd either walk or ride my horse over the pastures. I'd hobble my horse, Silver—I was into the Lone Ranger at the time—and climb over to school. I'd keep oats in a saddlebag and go out at noon to feed and water him."

Something about the look on Hunter's animated face fascinated Hannah, and she wanted to hear more.

"What did you do when it got really cold? I don't expect you left him to stand there all day."

"No. I gave in and rode the bus, but sometimes I took my skis."

"You skied to school? What fun! It must have been cross-country skiing, right?"

"Yes, but there are some pretty good hills in these pastures. Of course, if I went down one, I had to climb the other side. My teachers were a little touchy when that made me late for school."

"Well I don't blame them," she replied, indignantly, then giggled, spoiling the stern 'schoolmarm look' she had just given him.

Hunter had a sudden urge to lift her new cowgirl hat off her head and kiss her. He suppressed it, mightily. He turned back to the horses, and she followed.

"As to your question, it's a good idea to use the creek and field as a lab. Use the stile to get them over to it. Won't rip so many jeans or shirts that way."

"Thank you. We'll be careful. Of course, all the students will have to go. I can't leave anyone behind alone at the school. I'll just have to work out a simplified plan for the younger ones, and a more intricate plan for the older children. It should work."

She looked at him as he mounted The General. There'd been an odd look on his face back there. She hadn't a clue as to what had caused it. She hauled herself into the saddle, and Cinnamon followed them without being urged. The mare was doing fine, but Hannah figured *she'd* be a little sore in the morning.

They rode in silence for awhile. Hannah enjoyed her surroundings immensely. She reminded herself to put her observations into her journal that evening. The mountains to the east were beautiful; the blue sky overhead wide and handsome. She took a deep breath and sighed happily.

Hunter glanced at her. "What caused that big sigh?" he asked with a smile.

"Oh, I don't know . . . I guess it's just the mountains up ahead, the sky, the clear air . . . they make me feel happy. The sky is just so wide and open that I feel free, somehow." She grinned. "I'm not expressing myself very well."

"It's that 'Big Sky' feeling getting to you. We all see it and feel it at times. Sometimes, we get busy and forget to look up and around and appreciate it."

He did just that. He pointed suddenly, and Hannah followed his direction, as he said, "Look. There's a bald eagle."

"Oh!" she whispered in awe. "I've never seen one in the wild before. Beautiful!"

"Yes, it is. You'll likely see hawks, ducks and geese in the coming months, too, as well as songbirds and noisy magpies."

"I'll keep an eye out for them. I have a bird book in my school things. I'll read up."

They came to another gate in a fence, the second one so far, if Hannah recalled correctly. The new section of pasture was more level.

After he'd closed the gate behind them, Hunter asked, "Shall we try a lope now? You've been doing well. Just remember to try to meld to the saddle and move as your horse does. Push your new hat down tight, and let's go."

He laughed and it was infectious. Hannah felt a rush of adrenalin and urged Cinnamon to go faster. They closely followed The General, as Hannah felt he would choose the safest route. Though it wasn't a gallop, she still enjoyed the air whipping past her face. She managed to keep her hat firmly on her head and pulled up beside Hunter with a big smile on her flushed face.

"That was great! Poor old Starlight never went that fast. So, congratulate me. I stayed in the saddle and didn't lose my hat!"

"A toast to you, Hannah," he proposed as he took the cap off a canteen. He raised it in a salute, then handed it to her for a cool drink. She returned it to him, and he tipped it to his lips for a few swallows. "You're a good rider. With a bit more practice, you'll be even better." He recapped the canteen.

"Thank you. That's high praise from as good a horseman as you, Hunter. But I know that I still have a lot to learn."

"Well, we won't go any faster today, mostly because we don't want to stress Cinnamon's leg. But, if you come out alone someday, always carry a canteen of water. Some emergency granola or candy bars in your saddlebags or a pocket is a good idea too. A rope tied to your saddle can come in handy. High-topped boots aren't just for cowboy looks, either. They give your ankles support and protect your lower legs from scratches or snakebite."

Her eyes got huge. "Oh," was all she said. Then curiously, "Is that why you're carrying the rifle?" She had noticed it in its scabbard attached to his saddle at the barn when he had mounted The General.

"I don't always carry it, but yes, I kill rattlers with it if necessary. When I go up into the higher country, it can come in handy too, if I run into trouble. It's useful for signalling someone else, if you're down and injured. The men know to respond to a rifleshot."

"I'm glad you're educating me about it, but I don't think I'll feel confident enough to ride out alone, at least for awhile," she said seriously. The two horses walked side-by-side for a few yards; the only sound was the creak of leather rubbing on leather.

"Hunter, what about the rustling you and Fred Davidson were talking about?"

He looked grim. "That's another reason I'm carrying the rifle lately. So far, no one has been hurt—just rancher's pocketbooks. But the rustlers seem to be pretty cunning. There's been nothing left behind to give the sheriff a lead.

No tracks of any kind. No one has spotted suspicious activity. We figure they must have spotters watching a ranch, maybe even from the air, to know where and when is the best time to strike. But there's a lot of miles to cover on the area ranches and not many men to do it. Sometimes it's probably been days or even weeks before it's noticed that cattle have gone missing."

"I understand. I remember what Fred said about Chuck Carson's herd being up in the summer range. Is your leased land full of places where cattle could get lost too?"

"Yes, it is. Would you like to go up there? It's really rugged, beautiful country. You'll see first hand what Fred meant."

"Oh, yes! I'd love to see it."

They rode for another few minutes before they went through another gate.

"We're leaving the ranch now and entering our leased land. A mile on up, Cookie set up his cook camp near another nice spring. It's clean, but he boils the water first just in case, as animals can easily contaminate it. There's a narrow, dirt road nearby leading out to the road to Turk. Cookie used it to haul his chuckwagon into the camp."

"My goodness, a real chuckwagon? This'll be a treat."

Hunter laughed. "I think Cookie is going to like you."

Not sure what he meant by that statement, she kept quiet for awhile. Cinnamon calmly followed single file behind Hunter's horse as the trail led them through a pine forest strewn with large boulders. It was cooler in the shade of the tall trees and Hannah enjoyed the pine-scented air. Riding uphill on such a steep trail was a new experience for her, and she took care to balance herself properly in the saddle, thinking how foolish she would feel if she fell off.

When they drew up on level ground at the edge of a small meadow, Hannah smiled in delight. The meadow was ringed with aspen trees whose leaves quivered in the light breeze. The whole area sparkled in the bright sunshine.

To her right gurgled the spring Hunter had mentioned. To her left stood a wooden chuckwagon covered over with dusty white canvas. The tailgate was lowered forming a worktable of sorts. It seemed to Hannah that she'd ridden straight into a western movie scene, and she expected John Wayne or Clint Eastwood to ride up at any moment.

A few yards behind the chuckwagon stood a rather dilapidated, faded-blue pickup truck with a camper-top. It appeared that rust held it together for the most part. Must be how Cookie brought the wagon up here, she thought.

Cookie was on the other side of the wagon, but they could hear him singing at the top of his voice. The couple heard a rather bawdy sea shanty that Hunter quickly squelched by shouting, "Halloo, the camp!"

"Sorry about that," he murmured over his shoulder then prodded The General forward. Hannah followed.

Cookie rounded the wagon. A grizzled-looking older man with balding gray hair and a plump girth under his white cooking apron, he said, "Well, hello, Hunter. Good to see you. How are things back down at the ranch?" He stopped short and squinted up into the sun at the second rider. "Who's this with you?"

Hannah followed Hunter's lead and dismounted, though gingerly. The horses walked to the spring and drank, then foraged in the green grass near it.

It felt good to Hannah to be on the ground again. She just barely resisted rubbing the tender seat of her jeans. She walked forward and offered her hand to the old man.

Hunter introduced her. "Hannah Morgan, this is Cookie Bern, Clarence to his mother. Hannah's the new schoolteacher, and she's exercising Cinnamon today. Got a cup of coffee for us?"

"Sure do. Pleased to meet you, ma'am. Sit right down over here." He indicated a folding lawn chair, but she preferred to remain standing.

"No thanks, Cookie. I want to stretch my legs a bit. Coffee sounds good though." She smiled warmly at him.

Cookie beamed. "Coming right up."

Hunter chuckled and grinned at Hannah. "See what I meant? I knew he'd like you. You have a way of charming older men, *Ms*. Morgan."

"Really? If I do, I'm not aware of it, *Mr*. Grissom."

"It's your smile. You have a lovely smile," he answered in an aside as Cookie approached with two blue-enameled cups of his coffee.

Hannah was so surprised by his statement that she almost missed the cup's handle when she reached for it. She obligingly took a sip, nearly scalding her tongue, then set it on a nearby metal table.

"Good, but hot, Cookie," she explained. "I'll let it cool a bit." It was certainly the *strongest* coffee she had ever tasted.

Hunter, being more used to the brew, took a quick sip, then rolled his hands on the cup while he talked with Cookie.

"What's the word? Any sign of trouble?"

Cookie frowned. "No one's seen anything, but the guys are a little jumpy."

"How are the two new hands working out?" Austin Pike was the ranch foreman, but he'd only been with them for a year. Somehow, Hunter knew he'd get straight talk from old Cookie.

"They do the job, but they're kinda unfriendly to the younger boys. Sort of rough-edged, you might say. But the guys aren't complaining. Everyone's keeping their eyes open for trouble."

Hannah noticed that there wasn't a campfire and asked why.

"The fire danger is too high, Hannah."

Cookie added, "Yeah, I'm doing the cooking on two

camp stoves this year. Also having to buy bread at Whetstone since I can't bake biscuits in my Dutch oven."

"We're being more cautious of both fire and the herd than usual this year," Hunter explained. "Normally, Cookie stays at the bunkhouse. So do the hands, but they take turns, two at a time, riding up and checking the herd. They look them over, make a count, camp out one night, and ride down the next day. The herd usually stays on our allotment, as there's plenty of water and grass. Not too much wandering."

"So usually it's not such intensive work."

"That's right."

"Ever been on a ranch before, ma'am?" Cookie inquired.

"No, just on a wheat farm in Kansas. It belonged to my grandparents, and I liked to spend summers with them years ago." She unconsciously favored him with one of those smiles that Hunter had mentioned. Cookie beamed again.

Hannah picked up her coffee cup and drank more.

"Would you like some supper?" Cookie asked. "I can have it ready pretty quick."

"Oh, that's not necessary, Cookie, but thanks," she answered.

"Thanks for the offer," Hunter added then turned to Hannah. "There's a beautiful area on up that I'd like to show you, but it's getting late to ride farther."

"Yes, since we have the long ride back, and I've got to attend the teachers' orientation meeting tomorrow in Turk. I don't want to be *too* saddlesore!" Hannah laughed.

Cookie chuckled.

Hunter grinned and agreed. "We'd better start back down then. You've been doing so well that I'd forgotten you hadn't ridden for years. Can't have you unable to sit through those meetings tomorrow."

"Okay. It's been nice to meet you, Cookie. I hope to see you again."

"Thank you, ma'am. Ride up again sometime."

She and Hunter remounted and rode away with a wave. "So long," Hunter called over his shoulder.

The ride back took less time. Hannah attributed it to going mostly downhill, and the horses being eager for their supper and a rest. Ike came out when he heard the sound of hooves on the concrete floor of the horse barn. They led the horses to their stalls.

Determined to take care of Cinnamon herself, despite the soreness of some muscles and a certain area of her anatomy, she loosened the girth and swung the saddle off her back.

"Here, I'll take that," Ike offered. "I'll put it in the tackroom for you. It'll be ready whenever you want to ride again."

"Why thank you. I want to rub her down myself though," and she picked up the rags and curry comb Ike had brought to the stall. Working steadily, Hannah paid good attention to her task. She finished by giving Cinnamon a scoop of oats from the bin near the stall.

"Thanks, girl, for letting me ride you today," she said lovingly and patted the mare's neck. "I'm glad your leg's well, and I hope I can take you out again soon."

Hannah started at Hunter's voice. "She seems to be healed. I think she enjoyed being out again." He leaned his folded arms on the wooden divider.

"I think so. I gave her a scoop of oats. Was that okay?" She suddenly realized she perhaps shouldn't have done that.

"Of course. If you hadn't, I would have. Would you like to do this again next Sunday, Hannah? Without the after-church potluck, we can make an earlier start and ride farther up into the mountains."

Hannah was delighted. "Yes, I'd love it, Hunter. Will we be able to see that beautiful area you mentioned?"

"We'll head there for sure. Shall we go inside?"

Hannah closed the door to the stall behind her, and they walked to the house.

She intended to say goodbye to both Hunter and his mother there and drive home. But Elizabeth had supper cooked and in the warming oven, and Hannah gave in to her urging to join them.

"This is very kind of you. With the potluck at noon and supper with you, I haven't cooked at all today. I'm being spoiled!" She accepted with a laugh at herself.

"Nonsense," Elizabeth said with a chuckle. "Everyone deserves a little spoiling at times."

Hunter washed his hands at the kitchen sink, and Hannah used the bathroom to freshen up. She didn't want to go to the table smelling horsey. She rolled the sleeves of her red shirt up a few turns.

They sat down to hot ham, scalloped potatoes, and warm applesauce. Hannah was glad the wooden chair was cushioned.

"This is delicious, Elizabeth," Hannah said. "Lucky Hunter, he's getting his favorite warmed applesauce again."

"Mom knows how to keep me happy," he replied with a big smile for both ladies.

The conversation centered around the afternoon ride. Hannah mentioned how much she'd enjoyed meeting Cookie.

"He's a fine man and a good cook," Elizabeth said. "He used to be a cook in the Navy. When he retired, he returned to this area. Tom hired him about fifteen years ago."

Hunter gave Hannah a look. "That explains his vocal offering today."

She noticed the quirk of his lips, and she nearly burst into laughter. "I see," she murmured and took a sip of iced tea.

Elizabeth looked from one to the other. "Was Cookie singing again today?"

"Uh-huh," Hunter replied.

This time both Hannah and he laughed aloud. Hannah wiped tears from her eyes with a finger.

"I liked him a lot. He asked me to come up there again, and Ike told me the saddle would be ready for me whenever I wanted to ride Cinnamon. They're both such sweet gentlemen."

"Well, I wouldn't exactly call them *sweet*," Hunter remarked with another chuckle.

Elizabeth asked about the upcoming school year, and Hannah told her a little of her plans.

"I'm looking forward to getting started. I believe I must have met—from the list you gave me, Hunter—all the students at the potluck. Of course, I'm just going from memory."

"Actually, you're right. I think they were all there."

Elizabeth served a slice of cake to each of them, and they enjoyed it immensely.

"You're such a good cook yourself, Elizabeth. This is fabulous cake," Hannah remarked.

This time, Hannah insisted on helping clear the table and load the dishwasher.

"Now I'd better head home. I'll have to drive to Turk early in the morning for the teachers' meeting."

"Don't leave yet. I want to get something," Hunter said and left the room.

Hannah was curious as to what he was doing, then smiled when he returned and handed her a bottle of liniment.

"For your backside. We want our new teacher to be able to sit down on those hard chairs tomorrow." His hazel eyes were dancing.

"Thank you, Hunter. You're very thoughtful," she replied and giggled. "Is this for humans or horses?"

"Both. I hope you can manage to apply it by yourself," he added with a teasing, mischievous look.

"Hunter!" his mother scolded. "You should be ashamed of yourself."

"That's all right. I'll manage just fine." Hannah was surprised by his teasing. She was certainly seeing a different side of him today. She liked it. "Well, I'll be going. Thanks for dinner, Elizabeth, and thanks for the wonderful ride, Hunter."

"Goodbye, dear," her hostess said.

Hunter followed her outside. It was already much darker than she would have thought.

"It's getting dark earlier, isn't it?" She had left her house meaning to be home well before dark, consequently there were no lights on at the schoolgrounds.

Hunter seemed to read her thoughts and suggested, "I'll follow you home, Hannah. I suspect the security light isn't on, right?"

"Right. I thought I'd be back before dark. But, I'll be fine. Don't bother."

"No bother, just get in your car, Ms. Morgan." He opened her door and waited.

"Okay, if you insist, Mr. Grissom."

He shut the door behind her.

A short time later, she parked the car near the end of the path that led to her house. Hunter pulled in with his truck pointed toward the house. He left the motor running and the headlights on, then walked with her up the hill.

On the porch, she unlocked the door and turned to say goodnight. Instead he went inside ahead of her, flipped the lightswitch and looked around.

"Seems okay. Well, I'll be going. Have a good day tomorrow, Hannah."

She took off her hat and laid it with her purse on the table to her right.

"Thanks, Hunter. For the day and for this. It's above and beyond your duties as Board Chairman, I think." She smiled warmly.

"Well, I suppose so, but . . ." He suddenly swooped his head down and kissed her. One swift, warm kiss. Then he stepped back quickly. "Uh, sorry, Hannah. Hadn't planned to do that."

Hannah touched a fingertip to her suddenly very warm lips. Surprised, she answered, "I know. No need to apologize."

Neither spoke for an awkward moment, then Hunter muttered a quick goodnight and hurried out the door. The screen door slammed behind him.

Goodness! Hannah stood unmoving for a few moments, then went to the door. She heard his truck door close and saw the arc of the headlights as he backed around and drove away. She could hardly believe what had just happened. It had been unexpected, and she wasn't sure what to make of it, or him. They could be friends, but she didn't want to get involved romantically. Did she? Her heart was still too bruised from her ill-fated romance with Gregg Novak.

She closed and locked the inner door, then walked to the bathroom to prepare for bed. The liniment's odor was a little strong, but she wrinkled her nose and rubbed it in adequately. It was kind of him to think of it. She washed her hands thoroughly then brushed her teeth.

Climbing the stairs to the loft, carrying her jeans and sneakers, she told herself that it was wrong to even think of Hunter in a romantic way. He was her boss after all, and she wanted no complications while she was teaching here. She wouldn't kiss him again. "Shoot, now I won't be able to go riding with him next Sunday . . ." she murmured to herself as she crawled into bed.

Chapter Six

Hannah awoke the next morning still thinking about Hunter's kiss. It was *his* kiss too. It had happened so fast that she hadn't responded one iota. She definitely hadn't kissed *him*.

She threw back the bedcovers and stood up quickly. "Ouch!" she grumbled as she felt a twinge. The liniment had helped, but she was still sore. "I overdid it yesterday," she admitted to the empty room. "Shall I take a small pillow with me today?" She chuckled at that idea.

An hour later, she was on her way to Turk.

Hannah enjoyed mingling informally with the other teachers in the district in the lobby of the high school, then they went into an assembly where they were officially introduced to one another. She was pleased to learn that Whetstone wasn't the only one-room school in the district. Technically, Trinity School had two rooms. A husband and wife team, John and Barbara Winters, split the duties. Hannah was looking forward to talking with them.

The Superintendent of Schools addressed them, as did a well-known motivational speaker. Hannah especially ap-

76

preciated her thoughts on the course and future of education in the United States.

The high school principal spoke briefly, then the elementary principal added a few words. There was a luncheon in the high school cafeteria for all before they separated into individual meetings grouped by area.

By the time Hannah returned home, she was tired, but it was a pleasant tiredness. She had enjoyed the day. It had given her a mental boost.

One of the possible problems of the school year, having only one student in eighth grade, now seemed less formidable. She had talked with several middle school teachers about ways to bring out the best in that age group. John Winters had four students in the seventh and eighth grades. Despite being sixty miles apart, he and Hannah made tentative plans to get the youngsters together for a field trip or two during the year.

On Tuesday, Hannah made a detailed schedule of trips to their own outdoor lab. She wanted to begin immediately while summer conditions still prevailed. She had learned that first frost usually came around September 15th in the area. That would quickly change the conditions on their bit of creek and land.

She checked the sturdiness of the wooden stile. It was solid, in fact it looked like it had been repaired quite recently. Hunter at work? I'll have to thank him, Hannah thought. He's really very dedicated to the school. She climbed over the stile and explored the field and inspected the streambank and the stream.

Hannah returned to the classroom and put the finishing touches on pages that the students would use to record their observations. Over the months, they would put them into a notebook. She was grateful that the board leased a copy machine for her use, as she stacked the sheets according to their difficulty.

That evening, she wrote her postcards to people in Kansas. She e-mailed her parents, catching them up on the past few days.

The first day of school arrived. Hannah got out of bed more easily than the previous two days. After three nights of liniment treatments, her soreness had lessened.

After breakfast, she packed a lunch for herself. Working conditions were different at Whetstone School. No teacher aides, no free periods, no cafeteria, no relief teachers coming in to teach music, art, or physical education. Hannah was it. She laughed as she ran up the stairs to the loft. *I'll have to make time for an occasional trip to the restroom!*

In past years, her students often dressed up a bit more for the first day of school. Thinking these children would likely do so too, Hannah selected a pretty, pink-flowered, shirtwaist dress to wear with beige flats.

The bus was expected to drop off the children shortly before eight o'clock which made an early start to the day. The driver still had to make the trip into Turk with the older students from the area. Hannah walked down to the school, unlocked the door, went inside and gave the room one last look before the children arrived.

Hannah walked to her teacher's desk, opened her planbook, scanned the day's activities, and ran down the list of students' names. Hoping she'd recall the face that went with each name when she saw them again, she picked up a glossy, wooden apple from her desk. It had been a gift from her supervising teacher at the end of her practice teaching term. Hannah treasured it and had displayed it on her desk through each school year since.

Now she weighed it in her hand, closed her eyes, and prayed that she, the children, and their little school would be watched over from above. *Please, let me make a positive difference in their young lives, Lord. Amen.*

She opened her eyes as she heard a car drive into the

parking area. Thinking it was a parent dropping off a child, she hurried to the open door. Her stomach tightened when she saw Hunter's truck and Hunter himself getting out. Why's he here? she thought.

"Good morning, Ms. Morgan. Looks to be a fine day to start the school year." He smiled casually. He thought he should apologize to her about that kiss, but this wasn't the best time with the students arriving momentarily.

She hauled in a deep breath. "Good morning. Yes, it's a lovely day." She waited for him to explain his presence.

"I forgot to mention it, but I always come by the first morning to welcome the kids. Over the months, you'll have several visits from the county supervisor, but I like the kids to know that our teacher has closer backup, if needed."

So it wasn't about that unexpected kiss. "Oh. I don't anticipate any disciplinary problems, Mr. Grissom. But if this is a tradition, of course, stay to welcome them."

"Thank you. They're a good group of children, but a couple of the boys may try to test you. They did last year's teacher, I know."

"That's typical, but I'll stay on my toes. That sounds like the bus now."

Hannah walked to the porch and watched the children pour off the bus and walk, run, or race down the driveway. Hunter stayed inside. Hannah greeted and welcomed them as a group as they approached the porch.

"Come in now and put your lunch away in the refrigerator, if needed, or on the kitchen counter. Then please find the seat with your name on it. Lacey, will you help Nancy and Darcy find theirs?"

Lacey Gunderson, a fifth grader, was the first grade twins' sister.

"Sure, Ms. Morgan."

Hannah walked inside, and the students followed. Some of them spoke to Hunter as they passed him. He nodded and smiled.

When all were settled in their seats, Hannah looked around the room and gave them a lovely smile.

"I'm very glad to have all of you here. As you already know, my name is Ms. Morgan. I've written it on the chalkboard. I put your names on your desks so that I can learn your names better. Later on, we may rearrange the desks as we see the need for it." She glanced at Hunter. "Now, Mr. Grissom, our Whetstone School Board Chairman, would like to say a few words." She stepped back and Hunter moved forward.

He smiled and let his gaze roam around the room. "Good morning, everyone. It's a fine day to begin a new school year. I want to welcome you back and tell you that the board and I feel lucky to have found such an experienced teacher as Ms. Morgan to be with us this year. I hope it's a wonderful year for all of you." He turned to Hannah. "Now I'll be going so that you can begin your day. If there's ever anything I can do to help out, please call on me."

He smiled, put on his hat, said good-bye, and left to a chorus of "Good-bye, Mr. Grissom."

Hannah observed that he had done that well. Then, as a first order of business, she moved to the piano which she had angled away from the wall, enabling her to see the students as she played.

"I like singing and playing the piano, class. It'll be a good way to start the day. Does anyone have a song in mind to sing?"

She ran through a few chords, heard a few suggestions, and launched into one that she felt everyone would know.

"Three songs will be enough for today, I think. My, you sounded good. We'll have to learn lots of songs this year. By the way, does anyone else play the piano?"

Annie Clark, another fifth grade girl, raised her hand. "I do, Ms. Morgan, but I'm not real good."

"I'd love to hear you play, Annie. You choose a piece

and practice it, then you can play it for us one of these days."

The girl looked shyly back at Hannah, but nodded her head. "Maybe, Ms. Morgan."

Hannah smiled at her, then asked, "Does anyone else play a musical instrument?"

A few hands went up. Lacey Gunderson said she'd just started piano last year. A fifth grade boy, Mike Kramer, played the guitar a little. Charlie Carson admitted to playing the guitar and violin.

"I never took lessons, but my grandpa taught me."

One of the other boys said, "He's really good too."

Charlie looked embarrassed, but he agreed to play for them one day.

"Good," Hannah said to all. "We'll enjoy having our own musical programs this year. But let's not limit it to music. If anyone else has something to share with your classmates, we'd love to know about it. Perhaps you have a hobby you could share with us. Perhaps you have a much-loved pet to talk about. Perhaps you've been to a place you could tell us about. Perhaps something nice has happened to you or your family that you could share."

She paused. "That is how I hope you will think of the others in this room, boys and girls, as a family. An extended family outside your own home. A group of students who care about one another, who do their best with their own schoolwork, and who help their younger classmates to learn to do their best also. Over the years, you've gotten used to learning in a one-room school situation, except for our two new first-graders." She smiled at Nancy and Darcy. "But I hope you'll pitch in with an extra effort this year.

"Of course, we'll follow the usual coursework. We'll learn more in the areas of reading, writing, spelling, English, history, geography, and math. But, I'm looking forward to time spent on special activities, and I hope you will too.

"For example, one that I want to get started on tomorrow is in the science area. We have a wonderful opportunity here at Whetstone School that some city students don't have: our own outdoor science lab."

Hannah caught a few looks of interest exchanged. But little Nancy shyly put up her hand. "Ms. Morgan, what's a lab?"

"That's a good question, Nancy. Say, can anyone explain what a lab is to one of the younger members of our 'family'?"

Mike raised a hand. "One kind is a dog. Lab is short for Labrador retriever." He grinned. He knew that wasn't the kind of lab his teacher meant.

The boy seated next to him, Jack Hines, spoke up. "That's right, but the kind the teacher's talking about, Nancy, is short for 'laboratory'. That's a room where scientists study stuff."

"Thank you, boys. But instead of being in a room, our lab will be outside. It'll cover the schoolgrounds and a section of the pasture and creek across the fence from us. Mr. Grissom has given permission for us to study that part of his land. We'll climb the stile to get over to it, so on Thursdays, starting tomorrow, please wear older jeans and shirts and shoes, as we may get dirty on our trips to our outdoor science lab."

Hannah was pleased to see the happy expressions around the room. The idea seemed to go over well. And why not? Most kids love to get dirty! She giggled inwardly.

"Now, let's stretch our legs by coming over to the shelves and getting your textbooks and workbooks for the year. The usual rules apply, please keep your textbooks clean, don't write in them, and so on. We're fortunate to have several new readers and history books this year. Charlie, will you, as our eighth grade member, start us off?"

"Yes, Ms. Morgan," he replied. He came to the shelves and she handed him his textbooks and workbooks.

The day had gotten off to a good start, and it continued that way. The older students completed reading assignments while Hannah worked with the twins. She wanted to see how much prior knowledge they had of their numbers and alphabet.

Lunch hour was taken outside in the shade of two large elm trees. It was a pleasant time, and Hannah enjoyed the casualness of it. The children bantered among themselves as they ate, and it gave her a chance to further develop her impressions of their individual natures. As in any group, Hannah observed traits of shyness, bossiness, maturity, mothering, wit, and unselfishness. She made a mental note to have cookies or crackers and fruit on hand often. Some lunches were sparse.

After lunch, they had recess. The older boys went to an open area to play pitch and catch, as several had brought their ballgloves that day. Behind the building were swings, a slide, a merry-go-round, and a jungle gym. The others gathered there. Though the older girls mostly stood around talking, they did push the younger kids on the swings, or they got the merry-go-round spinning for them.

When the bus stopped for the pupils that afternoon, they and Hannah had had a very full day. But it had been a happy and productive day. She sat at her desk, mulling it over for a few minutes, then checked over tomorrow's plans. A major part of it would be spent in their outdoor lab.

She yawned and stretched. Getting up, she emptied trash into a garbage bag and carried it out to the large dumpster near the road. Back inside, she gathered a few books to take home, turned off the lights, and locked the door behind her.

I'm going to bed early tonight! she swore inwardly as she climbed the stairs to change out of her dress.

A few hours later, she was comfortably settled on her

couch, reading ahead in a history book, when the phone rang.

Wondering if it would be a parent with questions, she answered readily, but politely. "Hello, this is Ms. Morgan."

There was a pause, then, "Good evening, Ms. Morgan. This is Hunter Grissom."

"Oh, I thought it might be a parent calling. Hi, Hunter."

"Hi. How did the rest of your day go? Well, I hope?"

"Very well, thanks. I think I've a fine group of kids here. We got off to a very good start."

"I'm glad to hear that. Say, have you had dinner yet? If not, perhaps we could eat together? Mother is visiting a friend in Turk, and she told me I'd be on my own tonight."

Should I or shouldn't I? Hannah quickly asked herself. "Well, no, I haven't eaten. I've been lounging on the couch reading and haven't thought about dinner yet." She suddenly laughed. "Why, do you want me to cook?"

Hunter replied indignantly, "No, I can handle myself in a kitchen, thank you, but I just don't want to tonight. Eating Mary Jerome's good cooking at the Whetstone Store seems a much better idea."

"That does sound appealing, and as my stomach just growled, I accept your kind invitation."

"Good. I'll pick you up shortly. I want to talk to you about something too, Hannah. See you soon."

"Okay. See you soon." She hung up the phone wondering about his motives. *Has someone complained about me already? Surely not. Is that kiss on his mind?*

She freshened up, donned brown slacks and a caramel-colored pullover shirt, and stepped back into her flats. While she was in the loft, she laid out sneakers, socks, jeans, and a yellow teeshirt to wear to their lab in the morning.

Hearing Hunter's truck, she hurried downstairs. Grabbing her purse, she turned on the porch and security lights, before she locked the door behind her. He was halfway up the path when Hannah stepped off the porch.

"Hello," she called and walked to meet him.

"Hi, Hannah. You look nice."

Taken aback, she replied, "Thank you. So do you."

He was in newer jeans, a brown western-cut shirt, and the same boots and white hat he'd worn to church.

Hunter opened the truck door, and she climbed in with a little boost from his hand under her elbow. They arrived at the store and restaurant so quickly that neither had had time to say anything.

Inside, Hunter chose a table near one of the curtained windows. He held Hannah's chair for her, hung his hat on back of the extra chair, then sat opposite. She laid her purse on the same extra chair and looked around the room.

There was an older couple at one table. She smiled and nodded, though she couldn't remember their names. Two cowboys, eating their meals, stared curiously at Hunter and her. She figured they knew him but wondered who she was.

Hunter smiled across at her. "Don't mind them. They're just curious. Not used to seeing me with a pretty young woman, I suspect."

"Oh, well, I should get used to it, since I'm the stranger in town. Should I strap on a pair of six-guns?" She giggled in response to her own silly thought.

Hunter chuckled too. "No need. All the menfolk in these parts would happily come to the rescue of our new school-marm, if needed."

"That's nice to know," she replied with another smile.

Mary Jerome approached their table to take their order. They both chose the special: grilled pork chops, mashed potatoes, gravy, mixed vegetables, rolls and coffee. Hannah asked her to hold the gravy on hers.

After Mary had left them, Hannah sat back and asked her dining companion, "Now what is it that you want to talk about? Has a parent complained about me already?" She hoped that wasn't the case, but she held her breath for a moment.

"No, Hannah. Nothing like that at all."

She was relieved, but he sat staring out the window. She began to feel tense again. He turned back to her with a serious look on his tanned face.

"Maybe this isn't a good time to talk, after all. Too many listening ears. Later would be better."

Puzzled, she nevertheless agreed. "All right. By the way, your coming by to welcome the students back was a nice touch. I was surprised by it, but I appreciated the gesture."

Hunter smiled. "You're welcome. It's been done for several years, and I think the kids expect it by now."

"Did you mean it about being willing to help?"

"Of course." His look said he wouldn't have offered if he hadn't meant it.

"Well, we're having our first outdoor lab tomorrow. I've asked the children to wear older clothes for lab days. I plan to do it every Thursday for awhile. They were very enthusiastic about the idea, but that made me think, fourteen children, going every which way over that piece of land, and my having to help the littlest ones more." She paused.

Hunter inserted, "You could use an extra pair of eyes, hands, and legs, perhaps?"

"Yes. Do you know of someone who would be free to be an aide just for labs? At least on occasion."

"You bet. I'm volunteering."

Surprised, Hannah protested, "But surely you're too busy with the ranch right now."

"I can make time for something like this, Hannah. I'd enjoy it very much. Teaching has always interested me."

"I'll look forward to having your help then, Hunter. Thank you. I plan to begin about eight-thirty tomorrow. But it may vary other Thursdays. I'll try to let you know in advance, and if ever for any reason you can't come, just call me."

"Okay, that's a deal. Now how big an area are you planning to cover?"

She began to reply, but their dinners arrived. They ate some of their food before she went on. She told him that they would first cover the schoolgrounds, then go over the stile to his land. She gave him the perimeters as she recalled them.

"That sounds good. A fairly large area, but not too large that they can't get all over it in each lab session. I expect the creek will be a big attraction for all ages."

She grinned in response to his. "Yes, I imagine some feet will be wet occasionally. That's partly why I asked them to wear old clothes on Thursdays. By the way, I want to thank you for repairing the stile. I noticed it was much more solid yesterday."

"You're welcome. It's good that you aren't including that pile of rocks that's up the slope to the north."

"I thought it might be a bit dangerous to climb on. I don't want any broken bones."

"That's true, but I've also seen rattlers there other summers. There's probably a nest, and they come out to sun on the rocks."

Hannah paled in response to his statement. "Goodness. I'll make sure they know the rocks are out of our lab area then. Do you think I'm putting the children in danger by doing this? Somehow, it didn't seem dangerous when I first had the idea, but rattlesnakes change the picture."

"As long as the kids avoid the rocks, you should be fine. The rattlers won't come looking for them, but they wouldn't like the kids bothering them on their territory. I'll add a few words about that myself tomorrow, if that's all right with you, teacher?"

"Yes, please do that."

She used her napkin, and Hunter asked if she'd like dessert.

"That's tempting. Are you having any?"

"Let's see if Mary has peach cobbler tonight. It's always good this time of year."

Mary did, and they both indulged in a bowl. Hunter paid their bill, and they drove back to the teacherage. Hannah wondered if he'd now bring up whatever he'd wanted to discuss with her.

Still sitting in the truck, he began, "Hannah, I know I said I was sorry, but I feel I should still apologize for stealing that kiss the other night. I know it surprised you. To be honest, it surprised me, too."

She took a deep breath. "It was just unexpected, Hunter, and since you and I have to maintain a professional relationship, your being the board chairman and all, it didn't seem right. Not . . . not that it wasn't nice."

She looked out the windshield toward her house.

Hunter cleared his throat. "Yes, it was nice." He fell silent for a few moments. "I'm not sure I can explain why I did it. But I'd enjoyed riding with you that day, getting to know the young woman, not just the teacher we'd hired."

"I accept your apology, Hunter. It was a wonderful day. I'm hoping we can forget about the kiss and still spend some time together like tonight. It's been good talking with you this evening."

She paused, then gripped her hands together as she continued.

"I'm not interested in romance right now. I just survived a hurtful relationship in Topeka, and I want to get past that before I even think of getting involved again. Do you understand?"

Hunter sighed. "Sure, Hannah, of course I do. I've come through a couple of bad relationships in my day. I've put them behind me, but you need some time yet, and time does help. Is that partly why you decided to move to Montana?"

"Yes, that's the main reason. He's the principal at my old school, and I didn't want to remain on staff anymore." She couldn't bring herself to tell Hunter all the facts about the situation. They were still too painful.

He sensed that she wasn't going to say anything else about the past, so he suggested they call it a night.

Getting out of the truck, Hannah replied, "Yes, I told myself I'd get to sleep early tonight. It's been a long, full day."

"But a good one. Right?"

"Yes," she agreed, as they reached her door. "I'm really excited about this coming year too." She unlocked the door, and they stepped inside.

Hunter made a quick sweep of the rooms, as he had before, then said, "Goodnight, Hannah. I'm glad we talked, and I look forward to being with you and the kids tomorrow."

She smiled that lovely smile and extended her hand. "Thanks for dinner, Hunter. See you tomorrow."

Hunter shook her hand, then turned to the door. "I hope we can still go riding on Sunday afternoon. Cinnamon and The General are expecting you." He gave her a coaxing smile, and she laughed.

"Well, we can't disappoint *them*, can we? I'll look forward to it very much. Goodnight."

"Goodnight, Hannah." He disappeared through the door.

She locked it behind him. When she heard the truck start, she turned off the porch light, but left the security light on for the night. Not that she was afraid. It was just terribly dark outside. She was so used to the constant lights in a big city that getting used to the utter darkness was going to take time.

Chapter Seven

The next morning, Hannah walked down to the school early to do last-minute preparations for the first session of the outdoor lab. She placed a clipboard on each desk and pages on which to record information. She then packed a colorful canvas shoulderbag with a few emergency items.

When the students arrived, they began their day as they had on Wednesday. After a few minutes of robust singing, Hannah led them into a discussion of what she expected of their time outside. She printed on the chalkboard: observation.

"What does this mean, class?" She nodded at Charlie who had raised his hand.

"It means looking at something."

"Yes, it comes from the word 'observe,' which means to look or to see. In our lab we'll observe our surroundings and make notes on our lab pages. Now look over your pages to get an idea of what we'll be looking for out there."

She went back to the chalkboard. "Let's list things we will likely observe."

"The temperature," offered Maria Diaz, a dark-haired fourth-grader, who looked at the first item on her page.

Hannah printed. "Good. We have an outdoor thermometer to measure the temperature of the air. Mike, please go to the window and read the temperature for us all. Maria, would you sit with our two first-graders and give them some help at recognizing on their pages what we are talking about." Hannah had supplemented the written words with little sketches on the twins' pages.

"It says 51 degrees, Ms. Morgan."

"Thank you. Mike. Please write that on your first page in the proper place, class, then at the top of the page, put your name and today's date. Who knows today's date?"

Several children spoke up. "It's August 30th, I think."

"I think it's the 30th, too."

"No, it's the 31st, because yesterday was August 30th."

"That's so," Hannah agreed, "the 30th was the date of the first day of school. Thank you." She wrote the date on the chalkboard.

"Now look down the pages. What else do we find?"

As the students called out the different sections on their pages, she listed them, then discussed them for a few minutes to help enlarge their understanding.

"Please remember that we will observe *only* and write down what we see. We may touch the grasses, flowers, leaves, stones, bark on the trees, and such, but we will leave them there. After all, we want to see these same things in their same places next week and the week after that. We want to write down how the changing of the seasons makes a difference in what we see. Not touching any animals we may find is important also. Why, class?"

A few hands shot up eagerly.

Lacey said, "We don't want to hurt them."

"That's right, Lacey," Hannah agreed.

Joe noted, "We don't want to leave our smell on them either."

Being rural children, Hannah knew someone would remember that, though several others snickered.

Joe bristled a bit. "You know what I mean. If the mother of the animal smells our odor on it, she'll push it away."

"That's very true, Joe," Hannah said with a warm smile. "The mother wouldn't like the smell of a human. It could frighten her and cause her to abandon or leave her baby behind. We don't want that to happen."

There were a few murmurs of agreement around the room.

"So we agree not to touch any animals, but we will write down what we see, what it looks like, and describe what it's doing. Those of you who like to draw, take a few minutes to sketch the animal, or any other thing you'd like. Maybe the sky and clouds, flowers, leaves, and fish you see. Please, remember that this is *your* project and you can add anything to your pages that you want. My plan is just a place for you to start.

"The next time I go to town, I'll purchase a loose-leaf notebook for each of you to keep your pages together. Later on, we can look back through them and compare what we saw and how things changed. Also it's fine with me if you'd like to work in pairs or small groups. If anyone discovers something very interesting, call out so the rest of us can see it too."

Hannah glanced up as the outer door opened and Hunter stepped through.

"Good morning, Mr. Grissom," she and several of the students said.

"Morning," he replied with a smile. "Am I on time, Ms. Morgan?"

"Yes, indeed. We've been discussing what we'll be looking for outside. I was about to remind the children of safety rules."

He nodded and waited off to one side of the room.

"Please try to keep track of your clipboard and pencil. Don't run while carrying your pencil. Don't climb trees unless I give permission. I'll have a bag with me holding tissues, water, extra paper and pencils, and such. If you need something, just find me. If you have questions, don't hesitate to ask me or Mr. Grissom."

"Where all can we go, Ms. Morgan?" asked Tony, Maria's older brother.

"We'll cover the schoolgrounds first, Tony. When we're all ready, we'll cross to Mr. Grissom's land by using the stile. Watch out for each other, please, especially on the ranchland. Mr. Grissom will point out how far we can go on his land when we get there."

Hunter added, "I'm looking forward to helping out today, kids." He looked at Hannah with an expression of anticipation on his face.

"Well, gather your things, children, and we'll go outside." She smiled, grabbed her bag and went to the door. The students followed and quickly spread out over the schoolyard. They chattered among themselves and, typically, paired up with other boys or other girls.

The time passed quickly. The students looked here and there and under things. Hannah reminded them to also look up and record the sky and clouds. It was a bright day with a few scattered cirrus clouds to the east.

Most of her time was taken up with giving special attention to her first and second graders, all girls who stayed close-by and asked many questions.

Hunter gravitated to the boys while still keeping an eye on the area in general. He kept Hannah in his peripheral vision in case she needed him. He felt the students were behaving very well, but later when all crossed over the stile onto the ranchland, they grew more excited and more active. As predicted, the creek was a magnet.

Remembering what Hannah had suggested as perimeters, he gathered the children around and filled them in as to how far to roam.

"Stay on this side of the creek, kids. You can go under the bridge, but don't climb the fence. The land on the other side is part of the Pringle Ranch." He nodded at Josh, the grandson of Mr. Pringle. The boy grinned.

"We'll go upstream as far as that very large cottonwood tree and to the north as far as the back of the teacher's house. Then we'll come back down to the fence." He motioned in the directions he meant as he talked.

"That definitely means that pile of rocks near the top of that far hill is off-limits. Remember that, everyone. Snakes are interesting, and we may see a few water snakes in the creek. But you don't want to meet a rattlesnake head-on, and I've seen several rattlers sunning themselves on that pile of rocks in past summers. Do you have any questions?"

There were a few murmurs from the group, then Darcy, her blue eyes wide, asked, "Will the rattlers stay away from us, Mr. Grissom?"

"They should. But to be safe, since we're out on rangeland, just be careful where you step or sit. Rattlers don't like to be startled." To emphasize his point, he looked deliberately around the circle and caught the eye of each student.

"Thank you, Mr. Grissom. I'm sure the class will follow your directions and your wishes. We all appreciate your help, and your letting us use your land."

Hannah allowed more than an hour for this first exploration of the ranchland. It was enlivened by the sighting of an aforementioned water snake moving quickly through the water. Nearly everyone caught a glimpse of it, and Hannah noticed several sketches of it being drawn onto pages.

When the youngest girls observed something, Hannah printed their words on their pages. They then added their own little drawings of clouds, birds and late-summer flowers. Even though she hadn't really gotten a look at the snake, Darcy drew a squiggly line to represent it.

"I want to remember the snake, Ms. Morgan," she said shyly.

Later, a flurry of excitement occured when the older boys

found a large anthill, and the whole group gathered round to inspect it. While a couple boys took sticks and poked at it, enough to make some ants scramble, they remembered their teacher's warning not to destroy anything. They left it to look at again next lab day.

There was another squeal of excitement when a trio of girls spotted two jackrabbits on the opposite side of the creek. The rabbits perked up their ears, froze, and looked across at the girls, then leaped away into tall, dry grass.

Soon after, Hannah called everyone around her. "Let's climb over the stile and return to the classroom, kids. Take time to visit the restrooms and wash your hands, then we'll talk about what we've seen."

She climbed over the stile, then took the smallest girls' hands as they did the same and then jumped down. The others followed. Hunter was the last one over. Hannah had waited for him and walked with him back to the schoolhouse.

"Thank you, Mr. Grissom. This first time out went very well, and a lot of that was because of your help."

"You're welcome, Ms. Morgan. It was great. Their excitement can be contagious, can't it?" he said with a smile.

She laughed. "It surely can. It's always fun to see things through their young eyes. It makes things new again."

Hannah offered her hand, and Hunter shook it.

"I need to get inside. Bye."

"So long. See you on Sunday." His eyes twinkled at her. "It looks like the liniment did its job."

"It did." Hannah laughed and hurried into the school.

On Saturday, Hannah again drove into Turk. She explored farther afield this time and decided she liked the little town.

At the office supply store, she purchased fourteen loose-leaf binders in various colors, nearly wiping out their stock. She tucked the receipt into her wallet in order to be reimbursed later, then looked in the book area and selected two in the science field. Their subjects were ants and snakes. She already had several similar small reference books on other Nature subjects, such as birds, wildflowers, rocks, trees, and the weather. She felt in light of what they'd found on Thursday, the two new books would be useful additions to their reference shelf.

Hannah stopped at the post office to resupply her stamps; but also to greet the friendly postmistress she had met before.

"Hi, Tillie," she said as she closed the door behind her. The jangle of the bell on it had brought the older lady from the back room.

"Well, hello! Hannah, isn't it?" she asked with a broad smile.

"Yes, Hannah Morgan from Whetstone. I came into Turk to shop today and remembered I need more stamps."

Tillie filled her request and accepted payment.

"How did your first few days of school go, girl?"

"Very well, thanks. The kids are great, and the community has been very welcoming."

"I'm glad to hear that, but not surprised. Whetstone is a nice little place. I used to spend a lot of time out there when I was a girl."

"Really? I'd love to hear about those days. Say, is it near your lunchtime? How about having a quick meal with me at The Cowboy. I ate there last time I was in town, and I thought I would again. The owner was so friendly." Hannah hoped Tillie would accept her invitation.

"Why, thanks, Hannah. Yep, George Bos is an old friend, and he and Hazel cook up some fine meals. Since I close the post office at noon on Saturdays, I'll be free to go in a minute or two."

So, they walked down the street to The Cowboy Cafe and were warmly greeted by the owner when he took their orders.

Over their bowls of homemade vegetable-beef soup, warm rolls and large cups of coffee, Hannah prompted Tillie to tell her about Whetstone.

"I'll see what I can remember. The church was built sometime in the 1880's, I believe. You should explore the cemetery, if you're interested in family trees. Most of the present names are carved there. The Regolas, Davidsons, Carsons, Pringles, Smiths, Conovers, Slagers." She paused to sip her coffee.

"Not the Grissoms?" asked Hannah.

"I believe Tom Grissom is buried there. But the Grissoms are newer to the area. Tom and Elizabeth Grissom bought their ranch from the Slager Family years ago. Have you been on the Grissom land yet?" Tillie asked.

"Yes, Hunter Grissom is Board Chairman of the Whetstone School, so I've met him and his mother. She had me to supper my first night here, and he kindly allowed me to ride with him last Sunday afternoon."

Tillie smiled wistfully. "That's the same land Walter Slager and I rode on fifty years ago. You see, the Slagers had owned that ranch for many years. My parents and Walter's were friends, and Walter and I went to high school here in Turk. He was three years older than me. He taught me to ride. Those times together are some of my happiest memories. I loved him dearly, but we didn't date. He was just kind to his younger friend."

Hannah caught the glint of tears in the older lady's eyes before she went on.

"Walter, against his parents' wishes, enlisted in the Army after high school. The Korean War was bein' fought, and he wanted to do his part. We wrote pretty regularly for awhile, but several months later he was killed. He's buried in the Slager plot at that cemetery."

Hannah sighed and touched Tillie's hand. "I'm so sorry. How terrible for you and his family."

"It was a difficult time, yes." She dabbed at her eyes

with a clean napkin. "Later on, his parents sold the ranch to the Grissoms. With Walter not comin' back to take it over from them, they lost interest in maintainin' it. Tom and Elizabeth were quite young. I don't believe Hunter was born yet."

"Do you ever go out there, Tillie?"

"I haven't visited the ranch, but for many years I've occasionally stopped by Walter's grave with a flower. He liked lilacs in the spring." She cleared her throat. "So, that's how I know the Grissom place."

"Thank you for sharing that with me, Tillie. I think Walter was fortunate to have such a loyal friend." She finished her soup and sat back with her cup of coffee. "Can you tell me about anything else?"

"Well, the store has been there a long time. The present owners added that nice little restaurant several years ago. The school dates back about as far as the church, I believe. The teachers used to board out with different families through the year. You've probably heard of that custom?"

Hannah grinned. "Yes. I'm glad that I don't have to do that. Bea Davidson told me that Hunter's father gave the extra land for the teacherage, and everyone pitched in to pay for, build, and furnish it."

"Sometime in the late sixties, I think. Rumor was that they hoped it'd make it easier to keep teachers, but they still seem to change often."

"That's what I've been told too. So far—cross my fingers—I like it very much. Several people have warned me about the winters being bad, but I don't see that as a problem. I'm hardy," she added with a grin. "Say, if you come out to Whetstone before the snow flies, please be sure to stop by."

"I will, Hannah. I may pay a last visit to Walter's grave soon. I want to tell him my plans. You see, I'm retirin' in a couple of months, and I'm gettin' married."

Hannah's face lit up. "How wonderful, Tillie. Who's the lucky man? I hope you aren't moving far away."

"No, not far." Her cheeks pinkened beautifully and her eyes sparkled happily. "His name is Zach Knutson, and we'll live south of town on the Courter Ranch where he's foreman. He's a fine man, and we've been casual friends for many years, but only recently became better acquainted. Most people will likely think we've lost our senses to get married after all these years."

"Not me, Tillie. I think it's great, and I wish you every happiness."

The ladies finished their lunch and went their separate ways.

Hannah strolled by Jackson's Western Wear and windowed-shopped, then suddenly went inside. She admired the ruffled skirt again but resisted temptation. Since she was going to be riding Cinnamon regularly, it seemed, she decided to buy the pair of cowgirl boots she had tried on before. To her delight the sale was still in effect.

Her last stop was at the supermarket where she purchased a supply of apples, oranges, bananas, and pears. She planned to keep a fruit bowl handy in the school's kitchen for any of the students to take to eat with their lunch. She also stocked up on muffin mixes and ingredients for a variety of cookies. They would do some baking in the coming weeks. She reminded herself to check if anyone was allergic to chocolate, peanut butter, or any other foods.

Sunday was another hot day. Hannah wore a short-sleeved, scoop-necked bright pink sheath to church. She left her hair down, then at the last minute pulled it into a black Scrunchie at the nape of her neck.

When she entered the sanctuary, she glanced around for the Grissoms. No Hunter in sight, but Elizabeth was seated with two ladies her own age. *I shouldn't expect to sit with them again, anyway.* She slipped into an empty pew near the back.

In a few minutes, she was surprised that Hunter walked down the center aisle and climbed the few steps to the raised platform that held the altar, pulpit, organ, and the choir seats.

Hannah remembered that this was an alternate Sunday. Pastor Blake wouldn't be in attendance to lead the service. Hunter was in charge today. She wondered if others took a turn some Sundays.

Her question was soon answered.

The small choir entered singing and took their places on the platform. When they finished and sat down, Hunter addressed the congregation.

"Welcome. I'm pleased to see so many of you in our pews this morning, and I'm happy to be our leader today, my usual first Sunday of the month. Let's rise and sing #241 in our hymnals, "Just a Closer Walk with Thee.""

A familiar hymn to all, the congregation sang it with feeling. Hannah joined in with pleasure. She welcomed the chance to be a part of a greater body of worshippers. Back in Topeka, she hadn't attended church with her parents and sister this past summer. She hoped God forgave her for that, and somehow she knew He understood her reason. When the music ended, Hunter led them in a responsive reading from the back of the hymnals. After that, he asked everyone to stand and greet the others around them. Hannah shook many offered hands and responded to their words of welcome.

Hunter read a few announcements and asked if anyone else had something to add. There were several requests for prayer for ailing members and relatives. There was silent prayer for a few minutes, then Hunter led the congregation in prayer.

The service progressed with an anthem from the choir, the tithing, and message. Hunter incorporated things dear to the heart of a farmer or rancher. Gratitude for the abundance of the earth, stewardship of the land and animals, pleasure at being able to live and work with Nature. He related his own experiences of each day trying to remember to "take a closer walk" with the Lord, whenever he was out on his horse seeing to his bit of the Lord's good earth. He encouraged his neighbors to do the same as they went about their daily chores. Hunter delivered his message well.

Then he did something that brought goosebumps to Hannah's arms. He picked up his hymnal and sang solo that wonderful old anthem, "How Great Thou Art."

Hannah was thrilled by his rich baritone and the heartfelt delivery of the words. Near the end of the song, Hunter caught her eye. His look seemed electric somehow, and she felt pinned to her seat. *What an odd feeling!*

Then Hunter motioned for all to stand and join him in completing the hymn. That seemed to release Hannah. She stood, breathed deeply, and sang with the others.

As people filed out, Hannah attached herself to a group of women who were effusive in their remarks to Hunter, who was dutifully shaking hands and thanking the members. In this way, she managed to slip through without having to say much to him, though he quietly reminded her of their planned outing. She nodded and moved along with the others.

Back home, Hannah ate a light lunch and changed into her riding clothes. A little worry niggled at her, as she slipped on a slate-blue shirt, buttoned the cuffs, and tucked it into her jeans. She pulled on her new boots and walked around in them. *They feel pretty good, but maybe I shouldn't have bought them. Perhaps I should skip going riding with him. If any other man had given me that look, I'd think he was interested in me. But Hunter knows I'm not interested in a romance, so why would he look at me like that?* She sighed and went downstairs to brush her hair into a ponytail for the afternoon.

Hannah dawdled for awhile. She wanted to give Hunter and Elizabeth enough time to get home and have lunch before she drove over to the Big G. She was still uncomfortable with the look Hunter had given her, but she decided to disregard it and just enjoy the ride. Going up into the high country appealed greatly to her.

An hour or so later, Cinnamon and The General carried their riders over the rangeland and up the trail toward Cookie's camp. Hannah felt much better. Her backside tolerated the saddle well, and the conversation between the two of them was casual and friendly, nothing intense or personal.

Cookie greeted them as they rode into his cook camp. "Howdy, Hunter. Ms. Morgan. Good to see you again, ma'am."

"Hi, Cookie." She gave him a big smile.

He beamed and hurried to pour them cups of his strong coffee.

They dismounted and Hunter led the horses to the spring.

They accepted the offered coffee. Hannah let hers cool for a few minutes before she sipped. She had learned from her first experience with the cook's hot, strong brew.

She was pleased to find several of the cowhands in camp. They'd come in for a quick meal of beans, bread, and coffee. Hunter introduced her to the three young cowboys who all stood politely.

"Boys, this is Ms. Hannah Morgan, our new schoolteacher. Hannah, this is Travis Jerome and his brother Trace."

"Pleased to meet you, ma'am," said Travis, who appeared to be about twenty or so. His brother said much the same. He looked younger and more slightly-built. Both had black hair and eyes and friendly smiles.

"Hello," Hannah replied warmly. "Jerome? Say, are you related to Mary and Jim Jerome at the store?"

"Yep," Trace answered. "They're our folks."

"They're very nice people," she murmured, then turned to the third young man.

"This is Billy Cooper," inserted Hunter, who watched Hannah's smile affect the cowboy. *I guess it works on kids as well as older men*, he surmised.

Billy grinned shyly and said, "Howdy, ma'am, Most people just call me Coop."

"Hi," Hannah replied, "Short for Cooper, I expect?"

Travis added, "Yep, but he reminds us of the cowboy star, Gary Cooper, too—sorta quiet, most of the time." He gave Coop a little biff on his shoulder.

Everyone chuckled. Hannah thought the tall, lanky, sandy-haired young man with his shy manner was very likeable.

"Don't let us keep you from your meal, boys," Hunter said. "Ms. Morgan and I will go bother Cookie for a bit."

While Hannah and Hunter drank their coffee, Cookie offered them a plate of beans, but they declined.

"You've still got to feed Pike and the other men, or have they been in already?" Hunter asked.

"Not yet. When the boys go back out, I'll look for them to come in. You know what, I've got beef stew simmering. Stop back after your ride for supper with us."

"That sounds nice, Cookie. If it's okay with you, Hunter?"

"You bet. We'll be hungry again by then. At least, I know I will." Hunter looked at her and appreciated how well she fit in, as she handed her empty cup to Cookie with her thanks. *I still think she's basically shy, but she's probably learned to overcome it when needed.* "Well, Cookie, if Hannah's ready, I promised her a ride up to the waterfall this afternoon."

Hannah got up. "I'm ready. Hunter told me it's a quite beautiful area up there."

Chapter Eight

The beautiful high country did get rougher as Hunter and Hannah left the meadow near Cookie's camp and rode a narrow trail through rocks, brush and trees. At times, Hannah wasn't sure they were on an actual path, but then farther on she'd see it again. Hunter seemed to have no trouble keeping to the trail. It first climbed, then dipped down nearer a creek for awhile, before climbing again.

Hannah was thrilled with the beauty around her, though she paid close attention to her horse. She needn't have worried as Cinnamon was picking her way along sure-footedly.

Sometime later, Hunter crested a ridge and reined in his horse. Hannah followed suit and gasped at the sight below her.

"I rode this way so you could get the full effect of the view," he explained and moved his left arm in an arc, indicating the scene.

They looked down into a large meadow that to Hannah's untrained eye seemed about a half mile wide and much more than a mile in length. A meandering creek ran a gauntlet of willows down the length of the valley. The grass looked thicker and greener here than on the pastures down on the ranch. The hills on either side of the rangeland were peppered with aspen and pine trees of all sizes. Rugged rock outcroppings spired skyward at odd intervals through the trees.

Here and there, singly or in groups, were white-faced Hereford cattle grazing on the grass, drinking from or cooling themselves in the creek, or lying down resting. The sound of an occasional bawl or bellow floated up to her.

Hannah was amazed at the sight and said so. "My goodness, Hunter, there must be hundreds and hundreds of cows down there!"

"Well, I hope so," he said with a chuckle, "otherwise I'd be worried that we'd been rustled."

Hannah laughed. "It's just that I'm such a greenhorn. I was surprised at the size of the herd."

"It's at its largest this time of year. Soon we'll separate out the yearlings we want to sell and some of the bull calves. A few of the heifers may have to go to market too."

"So this is the time of year to sell. Is that so you don't have to feed so many over the winter?"

"Yes, that's one reason. You catch on fast for a city girl." He flashed a grin her way, then pointed toward the north side of the valley. "I see the boys coming back to work."

Hannah looked where he indicated and saw the three cowboys stringing down a lower path into the grassland. She saw no sign of the hands they were relieving. The boys separated and rode to the outer edges of the valley as they looked for strays that may have wandered onto the hillsides. She watched Coop herd a couple of calves back to the valley floor.

"I liked your three young cowhands. Really nice fellows."

"Uh-huh. They're good kids and hard workers. I feel lucky to have them."

"Where are your other men?" she asked as she looked to the far end of the valley.

"I figure they'll be along soon, when they know the boys are back from their meal."

"Does the valley have a name?"

"On the Forest Service maps it's called Willow Valley. This is the upper part of Clear Creek that runs by the schoolgrounds."

"So that's the creek I've seen as we've ridden. I didn't realize it was the same one. Where are the falls you mentioned?"

Hunter looked at her animated face, the sparkle in her eyes, and replied. "It's a few miles farther up. Do you feel ready to ride?"

"I'm ready."

Hunter and The General again took the lead. Hunter felt strangely pleased that Hannah was so enjoying the ride and exploring the land with him.

They backtracked, then rode down from the ridge on a trail that switched back and forth in gentle angles until they came out on the valley floor. It was an exciting experience for Hannah to be actually riding among the cows. She again rode to Hunter's left, as that was how Cinnamon wanted to do it. She returned the waves of the young cowboys as they spotted the two of them.

Hannah saw that Hunter was using the opportunity to inspect the herd's general condition as he moved among them. He occasionally crossed the creek to look over a group on the other side, then came back to her side.

"Are they looking good?" Hannah asked.

"Better than I could have hoped for, considering the weather this summer. They've put on weight and look generally healthy. Now I need to just hang onto them until it's time to herd them back down to the ranch."

She looked at him curiously. "You mean the rustlers?"

"Yeah," he replied. "The more time that passes . . . I don't know. I'm just afraid the Big G's luck may run out."

Hannah lightly touched his arm. "I sincerely hope not."

He glanced her way, then looked quickly ahead. "Thanks for your concern," he replied in a gruff voice.

They rode in silence for several minutes, then they saw the three older cowhands, the foreman Austin Pike among them, riding down the opposite side of the valley. "Stay here, Hannah," Hunter stated and crossed the creek to meet Pike at a halfway point.

Some women might have prickled at his command, but Hannah was willing to stay put. For one thing, the foreman and his two companions looked to be a rough sort. While Pike paid her no attention, the others stared at her. She turned Cinnamon a little so she wasn't facing them. She realized she was probably being over-sensitive. She was a stranger to them and out here on their turf. They likely just wondered who she was.

Hunter came splashing back over the creek.

"Is everything okay?"

"Pike says so. Let's go find the waterfall."

At the end of the valley, Hunter headed up a path similar to the one they had followed down into the valley. Below them to their left, the creek gurgled through a steep-sided rocky canyon. About a half mile farther, Hannah began to hear the sound of rushing water.

"We're getting close?" she asked excitedly.

Hunter nodded and soon reined in The General and dismounted. Hannah did the same. They tethered the horses, and Hunter led her under a pine tree and between some boulders to near the edge of the canyon wall. Twin cascades of clear water, sparkling in the afternoon sunshine, poured over a rocky ledge and dropped some thirty feet to the floor of the canyon.

Hannah's "Oh, how lovely!" was lost in the sound of the moving water. She put a hand over her heart and drank in the beauty of the setting.

When she turned toward Hunter, a smile of delight on her face, to thank him for bringing her there, she was surprised to find him watching her. He grinned as she mouthed the words, and he leaned down to say in her ear, "You're welcome."

They sat down on a flat rock and just enjoyed the sound and the sights. Hannah looked up at the blue sky and pointed. Hunter looked and saw the hawk she had spotted. They smiled at each other. He really wanted to put an arm around her shoulders, but he knew that would be a breach of their "friends only" relationship.

They stayed there for some time before Hunter motioned that they should start back. Hannah nodded and stood reluctantly. She was quiet until they reached the valley floor and the sound of the rushing, falling water was far behind them.

"Thank you again, Hunter. That was truly spectacular. Such a lovely spot, and to think, it's practically in your own backyard!" She laughed happily.

"And again, you're very welcome. Next time we'll go farther up where the springs that feed the creek are, but today I remembered that Cookie is expecting us for stew."

"That's right. In my excitement, I'd forgotten."

The return ride went quickly, almost too quickly for Hunter as he was thoroughly enjoying Hannah's company. She seemed to really enjoy both the ride and the ranch. She was interested in the herd and what happened to it. Of course, Cathy'd liked those things, too. His thoughts grew morose as he remembered that Cathy had especially liked the money they represented. Somehow, he felt that Hannah was different. In his heart, he hoped she was. That thought brought him up short. Was he set to make a fool of himself again?

Cookie greeted them warmly and soon they were seated at the metal table near his chuckwagon enjoying plates of beef stew, cups of his strong coffee, and thick slices of buttered bread.

"That was absolutely the best, Cookie," Hannah praised

as she unashamedly used a hunk of bread to sop the last of the savory broth.

Both Hunter and she refused seconds. "We don't want to eat the guys' portions. Of course, if you're offering dessert, that's another story." Hunter grinned at his old friend and employee.

"Coming right up." Cookie returned with bowls of stewed apple slices liberally sprinkled with cinnamon and laced with canned milk.

"Smells heavenly, Cookie," Hannah said appreciatively.

They had just finished when the three younger cowboys rode into camp. They watered their horses at the stream then tethered them away from the cooking and eating area.

After greeting them, Hannah took her and Hunter's empty bowls and plates to Cookie's washing-up spot. The boys filled their plates from his stew pot. He put a slab of buttered bread on each plate, then poured coffee for them. Giving the boys a chance to eat, she washed the dirty cups, plates and bowls in Cookie's dishpan of warm sudsy water and rinsed them in another pan.

"Why, thank you, young lady," Cookie said with a big smile on his wrinkled face. "Now you sit right down here and keep me company while I eat a little of my own cookin'." She sat in one of his folding lawn chairs and put her feet up. He soon joined her in the other with his supper plate.

Hunter, from his seat at the metal table, caught her eye and smiled. She smiled back. She felt very content.

Cookie asked, "How was your ride today? Less painful than last week's?"

Hannah giggled, then said in a low voice, "Very much less painful. I don't think I'll need the horse liniment Hunter loaned me after my first ride."

Cookie guffawed and nearly choked on a bite of stew.

Hunter and the boys looked their way, saw Cookie laughing, and returned to their conversation.

"Well, I'm glad to hear that, ma'am, and I'm glad that boy had the good sense to give it to you." He wiped tears from his eyes with his free hand, then finished his stew.

Hannah glanced at the table and wondered why Hunter and the cowboys looked so serious and engrossed in their conversation. Was something wrong?

Hunter listened as the boys talked. Coop said that lately his tallies of the herd were running fewer than Pike's counts. Travis agreed. He wondered if Pike was seeing more cows than he was, or if Pike was padding the tally.

"Do you think that could be happening?" Hunter asked.

"I don't know," Coop replied with a shrug, "but we're sure not agreeing. I don't want to accuse anyone of anything."

Hunter sat deep in thought. "Well, Coop, you've worked for me longer than Pike. So have both of you boys." He nodded toward Travis and Trace. "I'm yet to trust him completely. Like you, Coop, I don't know exactly why. Just something. Cookie says the two hands Pike brought on this summer are sort of rough. Not friendly."

"Yeah," inserted Trace. "They hang together and are always talking in private with Pike."

Travis added, "Maybe it's just because they're older and don't want to be around us much."

"That could be. They always take their days off together. I don't mind that. I'd rather take mine with Travis or Trace here," Coop said in his quiet way.

"Well, thanks for sharing this with me. We've been lucky so far, but you guys keep this to yourselves. Stick together and watch your backs. I'm wondering if maybe the reason we haven't been hit hard by the rustlers is because they're working out of this ranch. I'll see what the sheriff thinks."

Hunter rose and asked Hannah if she was ready to head on down. She was and after a round of good-byes, they mounted their horses. They were soon back on the Big G proper.

"You've been awfully quiet, Hunter. Is anything wrong?"

He hesitated before he said, "Nothing for you to worry about. The boys opened up to me a little back there. They expressed concerns about the rustling."

"Oh." She felt he didn't want any more questions, so she said nothing else.

Back at the barn, she unsaddled Cinnamon and took care of her for the night, while Hunter did the same for The General. Ike came out to take her saddle, and she chatted with him for a few minutes.

Hunter walked her up to the house.

She stopped by her car. "Tell your mother good-bye for me and that I enjoyed my ride to the waterfall. I don't think I should go in. It's a schoolday tomorrow, and you've got a lot on your mind."

Hunter smiled guiltily. "Yes, I'm afraid I do. Sorry that I haven't been good company this last hour or so."

"Don't apologize. It's been a wonderful afternoon. Goodnight, Hunter." She reached for the door handle, but he opened it for her. She slid behind the wheel and dug in her purse for her keys.

"Hannah," he began, then paused as he tried to form his thoughts. Then, he only said, "Are your outside lights on at the school?" When she replied in the affirmative, he added, "Drive carefully."

"I will." She smiled at him as he closed her door firmly, then buckled up and started the car. Giving a wave, she drove away. *That had been a rather strange conversation. I wonder what the boys said to give him such pause?*

The next week went by quickly. Each school day was busy with activity. Hannah felt she was getting a handle on her students' abilities and their personalities.

On Thursday, Hunter joined them for their outdoor lab session. The children were excited, as before, but they were also eager to go right to work on it. Even the youngest of the students seemed to understand that they were looking for new things, but also noting any changes in places and things they'd observed the previous week. Hannah was pleased.

Hunter lingered a minute to talk with Hannah as the students went inside to wash hands and settle into their seats.

"I'm afraid I can't ride with you this Sunday, Hannah. I've a stockgrowers meeting in Billings over the weekend."

"Oh, that's too bad. I'll miss our ride, but the meeting is more important—part of your work, you might say. Right?" She brushed some dust off her hands then smiled up at him.

He smiled back. "Right. It's a quarterly meeting, and I'm obligated to attend. Say, if you'd like, give Mom a call. She might like to take Strawberry out for a ride with you and Cinnamon."

"I'd enjoy that. Yes, I'll ask her. Thanks for the suggestion."

"Well, I should be going." He lifted his hat and ran his fingers through his black hair before setting it firmly back in place.

"Yes, and I have to get inside. So long."

"Bye," Hunter said as he walked toward his truck.

Hannah talked to Elizabeth Grissom after church on Sunday. The lady was agreeable to accompanying her on an afternoon ride. In fact, Elizabeth invited Hannah for a quick lunch before they took the horses out.

Later, when they were saddling their mounts, Elizabeth said, "This will be good for me and for Strawberry. Neither of us has been getting enough exercise lately." She chuckled and patted the horse's neck. Strawberry nickered as if in agreement.

"You lead the way, please, Elizabeth."

"All right."

As they passed the dam and pond, Hannah mentioned that Hunter had said what fun they'd had swimming there years ago.

Elizabeth agreed that it had been fun. "He . . . he didn't mention his brother?"

Her voice showing her surprise, Hannah replied, "Why, no. He just said 'we'. I assumed he referred to you and his father or some of the ranchhands, perhaps."

"That's true. We all enjoyed a dip in the pond, but . . . well, let's ride on to the spring, and we'll stop there to talk."

Hannah was certainly curious by the time they arrived beside the spring and dismounted. They left the horses to drink then graze on the grass. The women sat down near the spring. It gurgled a bit as it flowed from under a small rock shelf. A very pleasant sound, Hannah thought as she waited for Elizabeth to begin her story in her own way.

Elizabeth got comfortable and folded her hands in her lap. Hannah pulled up her knees and clasped her arms around them.

"Hunter was our firstborn but not our only child. Six years later, Hale was born. While he looks a lot like Hunter, though not as tall, his personality is quite different. He's always been carefree to the point of being lazy, never willing to put any extra effort into the ranch chores, a cut-up at school, no interest in going to college, loved to rodeo. In fact, though I haven't seen him in many years, I suspect he's still on the rodeo circuit.

"Hunter was everything Hale was not. I believe this led in part to Hale's jealousy of Hunter. He felt Tom favored Hunter over him, and he was probably right. While their father and I loved both our boys, Tom did turn to Hunter in discussing ranch affairs, and such. Hunter was interested and willing to learn, and as the elder of our two children, he'd be expected to take over the running of the ranch someday."

"Did the boys get along?" Hannah inserted.

"Yes, they did, for the most part. But as they grew older, Hunter was away in Bozeman at college most of the time. Hale chafed at being expected to carry more of the weight of the ranchwork. He loved riding and horses but not the everyday chores—looking after the cattle, fixing fences, and such. Boring work, he said. He and Tom argued a lot about doing his share.

"Hale was really pretty good at rodeoing. After high school, he wanted to try his luck at the pro rodeo circuit. Tom said no. He insisted Hale go to college as Hunter had done, after all, Hale could rodeo on the college team. Hale rebelled at that idea. He had dreams of earning big money on the circuit and didn't want to be bothered with more education.

"It all came to a head that summer after his high school graduation. Hunter had finished college by this time and was back home. Hale insisted that he wasn't needed on the ranch anymore and should be free to go. He and Tom had some terrible rows.

"Then one day, he cleaned out his savings account, came home, and packed up his things. A high school buddy of the same mind to rodeo drove into the barnyard with a horse trailer, and they loaded up his horse and saddle and took off.

"He did come up to the house to tell me good-bye, but I couldn't talk him out of leaving. I wanted him to wait to say good-bye to his father and brother. He said it wouldn't change anything.

"So, he was gone. Tom said 'Good riddance' but he didn't really mean it. It ate at him for months, until he had a massive heart attack and died. Hale's running away took a heavy toll on this family." Elizabeth pulled a tissue from her jeans pocket and wiped her eyes.

Hannah got up on her knees and took Elizabeth's hands in hers. "I'm so sorry. What a sad thing. Even after all these years, it must be difficult to talk about."

"Thank you, dear. Yes, it is." She gave Hannah a brief hug. "So the daily operation of the ranch fell to Hunter. Hunter handled it well, though I feel he had to give up a few dreams of his own at that time."

"He's mentioned to me that he had an interest in teaching once," Hannah added.

"Yes, he did, and he wanted to see a bit of the world, too. But, that didn't work out."

Elizabeth shifted and said, "I need to move a bit, Hannah. Help me up, please."

She did and the older woman stretched her back, before she paced for awhile.

"Did . . . you ever hear from Hale again?"

"No. When Tom died, Hunter tried to trace him with the help of the sheriff's office, but to no avail. He may not even know that Tom died."

Hannah got to her feet again, and they walked toward their horses. As they climbed into their saddles, she offered, "I'm sorry that you lost your husband and Hunter his father so young. You should have had many more years together."

Elizabeth murmured in agreement. "We'd been married twenty-eight years when he died. That's better than some, I know, but still . . ."

They rode back toward the barns in companionable silence.

Elizabeth thought what a wonderful young woman Hannah was to listen so kindly to her sad old story.

Hannah thought what a tragedy to befall Hunter and his mother. They had obviously suffered greatly. It had surely colored the path of Hunter's life ever since.

Chapter Nine

Several weeks went by. Hannah's pupils were progressing in their studies. There were days of hard work, interspersed with more relaxed ones.

On one such day, they had their first musical program when Charlie Carson brought his violin. They added to the festivities by having the chocolate chip cookies the fifth grade girls had baked the previous day. Hannah provided fruit juice to accompany the cookies.

Charlie played very well, and they ended their impromptu concert by shoving back the desks and dancing a Virginia Reel in which all ages could participate. Both teacher and students had a fun time.

The days also grew shorter. Most mornings frost was apparent on the grass, then the day would warm enough to melt it away. On one particularly cold day, they observed the first snowfall. A light flutter of feathery flakes that melted nearly as soon as they touched the schoolgrounds, though earlier snows in the mountains could be seen whitening the highest peaks to the east, west and south of Whetstone.

All of this was recorded on their weekly science lab papers. By now, each pupil had weeks of observations in their notebooks. It was an excited group of children that sighted a flock of Canadian geese on their flight south. Many, of course, had seen this before, but this year they took special note of it.

Hannah continued to see Hunter at church and on lab days. His enthusiasm for being teacher's aide hadn't waned one iota.

He and Hannah had taken a few short rides together on Sunday afternoons, but it was late in October when they finally rode far enough that she could see the three springs whose waters formed Clear Creek and fed the waterfall.

Hunter seemed quieter than usual on that ride. She asked him about it.

"Your mind seems miles away. Is it my boring company? Or something else?" She grinned across at him when they stopped to rest the horses on the ride back.

He caught and squeezed her hand—A bold move, as he rarely touched her. "Never boring, Hannah." He smiled warmly. "My mind has been on the herd and the rustlers. About one more week up here, then we'll trail them down to the ranch."

"You're concerned about their safety for this last week or so."

"Yes, theirs and the cowboys, especially the young ones. So far, no one has been hurt by the rustlers, but those three boys are bound and determined that nothing should happen to the herd on their watch. I'm a little afraid they could walk into a dangerous situation and be hurt."

"I see." Hannah herself felt worried for the young cowboys. She sincerely liked all of them. "I hope that doesn't happen, Hunter. I've noticed you're looking tired lately. Have you been giving up your sleep to come up here at night?" He looked away from her steady gaze. "You have, haven't you?"

He looked back at her, his jaw set stubbornly, and nodded.

"But don't say anything about it to anyone, please. I've been riding up at night to check for any unusual activity. I've been keeping my own vigil, you might say."

Hunter wondered how much to tell her. The only people who knew what he was doing were Ike, the county sheriff and his deputies. The sheriff had agreed with him that his theory about the rustlers working out of the Big G could be possible. Hunter had given him the names of the two newer cowhands to check out, but he hadn't learned anything about them yet.

So Hunter rode up to Willow Valley under the cover of darkness. He took a little-used roundabout trail, and kept vigil over the herd from a distance. A month had gone by, but he had yet to observe Pike or his two older hands acting suspiciously. They'd gone about their nighthawk duties when it was their turn, as did the three younger cowboys.

He continued, "Not even Cookie knows about it, and the fewer that know, the better."

"Of course, I won't say anything, but you be careful yourself." When he didn't respond, she added, "Promise now, Hunter."

He arched an eyebrow. "I promise, ma'am." He pulled the brim of her cowgirl hat down over her eyes. "I'm always careful."

"Good!" She pushed her hat back into place and patted his arm.

Hannah meant to send her family and friends in Topeka some photos of her area of Montana, but she forgot several times to do it. She began by taking some inside and outside shots of her house and the school.

On Thursday of that week, when Hunter came by to help with the lab, she and her students posed in a group near the stile, and he took a couple of shots. Then Charlie insisted on taking the camera while Hunter got into the photo. He stood beside Hannah at the end of the back row.

Charlie urged, "Move in closer everybody."

So they all scrunched together. Hunter accomplished that by slipping his left arm around her waist. Hannah didn't react, but she admitted to herself that she enjoyed that slight embrace.

The next day Hannah received a letter from her younger sister, the first one since her move to Whetstone. She opened it with some trepidation, as she wondered what Heidi had to say that couldn't be put into an e-mail.

Hannah sat curled up in a corner of her sofa to read.

Heidi began with the usual niceties. Then came the news Hannah had dreaded. Heidi and Gregg were to be married over the Christmas break from school. She hoped that Hannah would be free to come to Topeka at that time. Under the circumstances, she wouldn't ask her to be in the wedding party, but she hoped her only sister would be able to attend the ceremony. Their parents and grandmother missed her, and it would be a chance to see them, too.

Tears ran down Hannah's cheeks by the time she'd read the remainder of the letter. *Why am I crying? This isn't unexpected, by any means.* She supposed just the finality of their setting a date and making preparations depressed her. She would have to make a decision about attending but not at this very moment. She laid the letter aside, wiped her eyes with a tissue, and picked up some class papers to grade.

She ate little that evening and tossed and turned when she tried to sleep.

Saturday morning brought chilly air but sunshine. Hannah felt the need to do something physical, so she donned her riding jeans, her boots, and a lined denim jacket over her T-shirt and blouse.

This wasn't her usual riding day, but perhaps Hunter wouldn't mind her taking Cinnamon out.

She put on her cowgirl hat with the red feather, and

pocketed brown leather gloves. She soon arrived at the Big G and parked in her usual spot.

When she knocked on the porch door, there was no response, so Hannah walked down to the horse barn.

"Ike, are you here?" she called, and he soon stepped through the door that led in from the corral at the far end of the aisle.

"Howdy, Hannah."

"Hi, Ike. No one's up at the house. Is Hunter around? I was hoping he'd let me ride Cinnamon this morning."

"Hunter's not here. He went into Turk, and Elizabeth's visitin' old Mrs. Adams who's been feelin' poorly."

"Well, may I ride for awhile anyway, Ike? I'd really like the exercise. Maybe Cinnamon would, too." She smiled at him coaxingly.

He gave in. "Sure, I guess you and Cinnamon know each other well by now. You've been ridin' her for about two months."

"Yes, it's been that long already. Thanks."

Ike brought out the saddle and blanket he kept on hand for her, and she soon had the horse ready.

"Hunter always carries water when he's ridin' out, so you take this canteen for yourself." He hung it over the saddlehorn.

"Thanks, Ike. I appreciate that. Hunter told me to always take granola bars or chocolate with me." She patted her jacket's breast pocket. "Right in here."

She walked Cinnamon down the aisle and through the door. Outside, she climbed into the saddle with much more ease than two months ago.

She waved as Ike came to the open door. "I'll be back in a couple of hours, Ike."

"Maybe you shouldn't go too far," he cautioned.

"Just up to the waterfall. I want to take some pictures. See you."

She was gone before Ike remembered Hunter's caution over the rustling danger.

He mused for a minute, then decided since it was broad daylight and the cowboys were up there, she'd surely be fine. He returned to his chores.

Hannah's first stop was Cookie's camp. He was glad to see her, and they chatted for awhile. He had a meal ready for the cowboys, but no one had come in as yet. He offered her a plate, but she declined.

"Perhaps, I'll stop by on my way out, Cookie. I remembered to bring my camera, and I want to ride up to the waterfall and take some photos. That reminds me." She hurried to the saddlebag on Cinnamon where she'd stashed her camera. Though Cookie seemed embarrassed by her taking his picture, she got some good shots of him and his chuckwagon. He returned the favor by snapping her atop Cinnamon.

"Thanks, Cookie! See you later." She waved as she rode away.

As she now knew the trail up to Willow Valley well, she made good time and was soon riding its length, carefully keeping to the south side and away from the Herefords. She didn't feel as confident riding among them as she did when Hunter was with her, but she paused to take a few photos of the herd and the valley. The now leafless willow branches added a starkness to her shots and reminded her that winter was closing in quickly. Hunter would be bringing the herd down to the ranch very soon.

Though she watched for the cowboys, she saw no one, neither the boys nor the older men. *Odd. I've never come up here when I haven't seen someone.*

Cinnamon and she steadily climbed up out of the valley and onto the trail that paralleled the canyon rim. A smile flitted across her face when she heard the rushing water. The sound grew louder as she neared the place where she and Hunter usually stopped.

She tethered Cinnamon and took some shots of the falls and the surrounding boulders and trees.

Hannah sat on the flat rock and let her mind wander. Perhaps, that was why she had really come up to the falls. Though she wanted the photos, she also wanted a peaceful spot to think.

Though she had shed tears last night, she suspected they were more because of the finality of the wedding plans than a lingering love for Gregg Novak.

Hannah and Gregg had dated casually nearly from the beginning of the last school year. He was hired as the new principal of her elementary school; she was the only single female on staff. She later wondered if he would have even asked her out if that hadn't been the case. But he was witty, nice-looking, intelligent, and she found herself more and more attracted to him.

When he showed signs of becoming serious about her, she took him home to meet her family. Heidi had left the house earlier to meet friends for a movie. Their parents liked Gregg. He used his considerable charm on her mother and talked seriously with her father.

The next day on the phone, her mother told her how much they liked "her young man" and asked her to invite him for dinner the next Saturday. She did, and he accepted, marking the beginning of the end of their budding romantic relationship.

Heidi was home that evening to join them for dinner and to meet Hannah's new boyfriend. Hannah's stomach cramped just remembering how many fellows Heidi had lured away from her over the years, from grade school to the present. It had never been pleasant being the plainer, older sister.

Hannah sat beside Gregg with her parents at either end of the table. Heidi sat across from Gregg and flirted with him, though Hannah couldn't be sure if she even knew she was doing it. Flirting came as naturally as breathing to Heidi. Gregg was obviously not immune to it. Hannah, as usual, felt tongue-tied and inept in the presence of her sister's sparkling personality.

She wouldn't try to deny that Heidi was beautiful. She had always been lovely with bright blue eyes and wavy long, blond hair. Somehow, she had never gone through a period of awkwardness as Hannah had. She had poise, and always sensed just the correct thing to say to make those around her laugh and feel at ease. Everyone but Hannah. Hannah always closed up in social situations when Heidi was around.

That evening at her parents' home was no exception. Her mother seemed not to notice Heidi's monopolizing of Gregg, but then she had always doted on her younger daughter.

As Hannah sat there through that interminable dinner, she thought of that, about how at age fourteen she had cried on her Grandma Withers' shoulder about the unfairness of it all, and her grandmother had tried to help her understand.

"Grandma, I've always tried to be a good girl, but . . . but they seem to love Heidi more. At least my mommy seems to. I've wondered what's wrong with me so many times. Why I'm so plain and Heidi's so pretty."

"Now, now, dear. Don't fret. You're a fine, bright, and caring girl, and I think you're pretty too. There are many kinds of beauty on this earth, and you carry the important kind. There's nothing wrong with you, Hannah, and I know your parents love you very much. You've surely noticed among your friends and classmates that all sisters don't look alike, just as all brothers don't. In your case, you favor your father's side of the house, in fact you look a lot like his older sister, your Aunt Vera. Have you ever noticed that?"

"No, but she lives far away, and I haven't seen her much."

"Yes, that's true. But she's a fine lady who married a minister and is a wonderful help to him in his work, I'm sure."

"So, it's just that I take after daddy's sister, and Heidi takes after mommy. Mom's beautiful. Heidi's lucky to look so much like her," Hannah said resignedly.

Grandma Withers hugged her where she sat beside her on the sofa.

"Now you just continue to be the brave, sweet girl that you are. Remember that I love you very much, too."

"I love you too Grandma. Thank you."

Hannah was brought back to that fateful dinner party by the memory of her father's hand on her forearm. The others were laughing at something Heidi had said.

"Please, pass me the potatoes, dear." He looked kindly into her troubled eyes, and added in a lower tone, "Pay them no mind, Hannah, for if he can be swayed so easily, he doesn't deserve you."

She returned his look and a flicker of a smile moved her lips. She mouthed the words "thank you" and handed him the serving bowl.

Gregg never had actually broken it off with her, she recalled, as she shifted on the hard rock. He just became less and less a part of her life over the next weeks after that evening. By the time he asked Heidi out, he and Hannah hadn't so much as gone to a movie together for a month.

But it still hurt, and it was painful to endure the whispers and glances of some of the other employees at her elementary school. Her true friends there were supportive, though, and that helped immensely. She managed to maintain a professional attitude when circumstances brought Gregg Novak and her together, but she stayed away from her parents' home more and more, not wanting to run into him there.

She and her father had lunch several times over the next

few months, and he understood her feelings completely. So, when at the end of the school year, she mentioned that she wanted to move on to a different school, he agreed.

"That seems like a wise choice, Hannah. You're a fine teacher, and you should have no problem finding a new position. It does seem that Heidi and Gregg may make a go of it. She speaks glowingly of him, and they go out often. Time will tell." He fiddled with his coffee cup before looking directly at her. "Your mother is complaining that you don't come home often enough. I swear, that woman can be as dense as they come. Why I put up with it . . ."

Hannah's hand closed over his. "Dad, you put up with it, because you love her. I love her, too. I love Heidi, but I just can't be around her right now. For several months, I thought Gregg could be the man for me, but that's not going to happen. It's just too hard to watch Heidi's happiness when I'm feeling miserable."

She gave him a bright smile. "But, I'll get over that. I won't let this discourage me either. Perhaps, there's a good man out there for me yet."

"I know there is, Hannah, and when you find him, this will all fade away." He lifted her hand and kissed it. "I love you, girl," he said with feeling.

"Daddy, I love you." A single tear escaped down a cheek, and she quickly dashed it away before he saw it.

Hannah stretched her arms over her head and ended her reverie. She got up and walked to where Cinnamon stood patiently and remounted. She glanced at the leaden sky. The wind had come up. She tugged her jacket closer and fastened all the snaps. The bright sunshine of an hour ago had disappeared completely. *Brrr! I should start back.* But, deciding she'd first take a picture of the three springs, she guided the horse in that direction.

She thought about Heidi's letter, and she realized that attending the wedding could be a positive thing. She certainly wanted to see her parents and Grandma Withers again. It would be an opportunity to see if she still harbored lingering feelings for Gregg. Somehow she doubted it. Her life had become so busy with school, church, and local activities, she rarely even thought of Gregg or Heidi anymore.

She had made many friends in the area. Being an honest person, she knew that the people on the Big G were largely responsible for her new contentment. Especially Hunter. She chuckled to herself. Yes, he'd become an important part of her life. But, she couldn't let their relationship grow at this time. She had told him she wasn't looking for romance, and he seemed to accept that. What would he say if she rescinded that statement?

All the more reason to attend the wedding. She had to know how seeing Gregg again would affect her. She had to be fair to Hunter. Of course, maybe Hunter wasn't as fond of her as she was of him.

Now that's a discouraging thought!

Suddenly, Cinnamon slowed and pranced a little.

"What is it, girl?" Hannah whispered and patted the horse's neck to calm her. She assumed the horse had heard something—something that her rider had missed.

Hannah looked around, her heart beating faster. There! Off to the left and ahead of them. Another horse nickered, and there was another sound she couldn't immediately identify. She crossed the narrow stream just before the three springs, forgetting for the moment that she had wanted to photograph the setting.

Chapter Ten

Hannah knew she was venturing into uncharted territory. Hunter and she never rode farther than the springs. But she let Cinnamon pick her own way toward the sound they both had heard.

When Hannah recognized it as cattle moving, she got off the horse and led it with a quieting hand on Cinnamon's muzzle. She hoped she wouldn't nicker, but the sound of the cattle could drown it out if she did.

This perplexed Hannah. She guessed she was about four miles away from Willow Valley where the herd grazed. Where had these cows come from? Had they strayed from the main herd? Maybe gotten lost up here in this rough country?

She heard a sudden shout over the bawling of cattle and the trampling of hooves. It caused her to stop in her tracks. *That was nearby. I'm not alone up here!* An apprehensive quiver went down her back, and she stepped closer to Cinnamon.

Idiot! she told herself and breathed a sigh of relief. *That's why the cowboys weren't in the valley when I passed through; they're up here rounding up strays.*

Deciding she could take some interesting pictures of that,

127

she tied Cinnamon's reins to a tree branch, then pulled her camera from the saddlebag. "I'll be back soon, girl," she murmured to the horse.

Hannah ducked under the low branches of the tree and carefully edged around a prickly shrub and between two large boulders. The sounds came from below her, so she knew she was above the stray cattle. She halted as she neared the edge. It dropped off steeply, so she left some waist-high rocks between her and the precipice.

She peered over the rocks and down into a large coulee. The cattle's hooves had churned up a cloud of dust, but she could make out about fifteen head of varying ages and sizes. The cattle appeared agitated, anxious to move, but Hannah saw the two older cowhands on horseback with lariats in hand. They circled the cattle and kept them in check. The younger cowboys—Travis, Trace, and Coop— were nowhere in sight.

Hannah was glad she had stayed hidden behind the rocks. She wasn't comfortable around the older hands. She aimed and snapped a few shots of the men and milling cows.

She started when, above the sound of the noisy cattle, one of the men shouted, "Hurry up, Pike. Jack's waiting with the truck."

Hannah's eyes darted across the coulee. With an effort, Pike lifted a metal gate and shoved it behind some rocks and bushes. He threw pine branches and rocks over it, but at this point it was not quite obscured from Hannah's view. It had blocked the narrow outlet of a canyon. She quickly took a picture of Pike as she hoped she wasn't too far away for it to turn out well.

Her mind raced. She had definitely stumbled into the middle of something. Why did they have a truck waiting? Who was Jack? Not one of Hunter's employees, she was sure.

It suddenly made sense, and she clamped a hand over her mouth to contain her gasp. She dropped down out of

sight behind the rocks. Hunter's own cowhands, the foreman Pike included, were rustling the Big G cattle! Not the
whole herd, but some they'd hidden away up here. She bet
they'd been doing it for weeks, slowly, so they wouldn't
be missed. *What should I do*?

Hannah realized she couldn't confront them. One woman
against three men? *Who am I kidding*? Looking again, she
saw that each man carried a rifle on his saddle. She looked
down at her camera and realized that she too was armed.
She had already caught them on film. Would anyone believe that they weren't just rounding up strays? Yes, they
would. This was too far away from the herd for the cows
to have "wandered off," and she had Pike covering up the
gate. A gate that looked very much out of place up there.

Her next thought was to see where they planned to take
the stolen cattle. Cinnamon and she could follow them at
a discreet distance. But then Pike mounted his horse and
grabbed the loose reins of another, one that Hannah hadn't
noticed before.

"That should cover it up for now. I'll come back another
day and haul it out of here." Pike added with a laugh,
"Won't need it again for awhile."

"Yeah, this has been a sweet little set-up. Almost hate
to see it end," the thinner of the two hands, aptly called
Skinny, agreed.

The other man, one that Hannah knew as Carney, asked
Pike, "Is he hid good?" He had an anxious look on his
mustachioed face.

"Yeah, don't worry. No one'll find him 'til long after
we're gone. We'll take his horse with us, and Grissom'll
just think the kid got tired of workin' and took off."

His rough words were met with laughter from his two
companions.

But still, the anxious one urged speed. "Let's get this
load to the truck before the other two kids come back out
from cook camp."

Hannah's heart beat even faster. Who are they talking about? It had to be one of the younger boys. She peeked again at the spare horse being led by Pike behind the now moving cattle. The hands were herding them up a narrow track away from the coulee. *Oh, no! That's the horse Coop always rides! What had they done to that boy?*

Hannah stood there, stunned by what she had seen and heard. As Pike rode out of sight, she pulled her thoughts together.

The rustlers, as she now thought of the three men, hadn't bothered to cover their tracks. She wondered why, as Hunter had told her the area ranchers had never found tracks on their land after being hit by the rustlers. When she felt a snowflake brush her face and looked up at the sky, she knew why. It had started to snow. In just a few minutes, the rocks around her and the ground below turned white. The fresh snow was covering their tracks for them.

She abandoned her idea of following the men so she could see the truck and its driver. Even if Hunter lost his cattle, there was a more important thing for her to do: find Coop.

She prayed he wasn't already dead, as Pike had implied. But, if someone didn't find him before the snow got worse and the air even colder, he surely would die.

Hannah retraced her steps to Cinnamon, put her camera into a saddlebag, and swung herself into the saddle. The horse was frisky, and her rider knew the sensitive animal felt her agitation and uncertainty. *Which way should I go?* Hunter was away from the ranch in Turk. Ike was all the way back at the barn; Cookie was miles away and without a horse; the Jerome boys weren't in Willow Valley earlier.

She started to ride back to the valley but stopped. By the time she found Travis and Trace, it could be too late for Coop. She'd do this herself. She gave Cinnamon her head and urged her to find a way down into the coulee. The horse was up to the task, and they were soon crossing the coulee toward the place where Pike had hidden the metal gate. He had come out of the canyon. That was where they had obviously hidden the rustled cattle.

She rode through the opening, only about four feet wide, and into a narrow canyon. It soon opened out into a steep-sided box canyon. Hannah had heard of box canyons before, and this was a perfect example. It was about a thousand feet wide and stretched half a mile into the distance, though she couldn't be sure with the snow obscuring her vision.

Hannah felt that Coop must have stumbled on the hiding place at the wrong time, and one of the men had possibly hit him to shut him up. Or worse. She had to find him, but she dreaded what she'd find.

She recalled Pike "had hid him good," and since he'd hidden the gate with pine branches and rocks, perhaps he'd done the same with Coop. She rode down the middle of the canyon and looked left and right. There was a clump of bare willows ahead. She was surprised to find a pool of spring-fed water nearby, which explained how the rustlers had watered their stolen cattle. She found no sign of Coop. *Hurry, Hannah,* she told herself, *the boy has to be in here somewhere!*

There were small stands of aspen and pine trees among the rocks along the outer edges of the canyon. She made the quick decision to check them as a possible hiding place. Cinnamon and she swung to the right and examined each area carefully before moving on to the next.

They were nearly back to the entrance when she spotted a large lump under a huge pine tree. It had a light blanket of snow covering it. *Could that lump be Coop?* Hannah stared at it and bit her lower lip. Taking a deep breath to calm her galloping heart, she swung out of the saddle and approached it.

"Coop?" she almost whispered, then louder, "Coop?" Her breath hung in the cold air as if her words had frozen.

Hannah heard nothing but the wind in the pine trees and Cinnamon snorting. She gingerly pulled away a branch from one end of the pile, then another.

She gasped and stopped. There was the heel and spur of a well-worn cowboy boot sticking out from under the rest of the branches.

"I've found him!" she shouted and Cinnamon responded with an excited nicker.

Working quickly, Hannah pulled away more branches until she could see Coop's upper body. "Please, Lord, let him still be alive," she prayed. She knelt beside the young cowboy and laid her right ear on his chest. At first she despaired but then heard, or perhaps felt, a slow heartbeat. "Thank you," she whispered.

She said his name a few more times, but he didn't respond. She was afraid to move him in his unconscious state, so she first felt around his head. His hat was missing, and she found a bump on the back of his head. When she took her hand away there was a stickiness on her leather glove. She looked and saw that the pine needles under his head were dark with blood.

He'd hit his head on a rock, or someone had hit him *with* a rock, she surmised. Hannah found no other injury to his body. She had been worried he'd been shot or stabbed. But when she looked at his legs, it was obvious his right was broken. It lay in an awkward position, his boot turned out at an unnatural angle.

Hannah knew he needed medical attention fast. He also needed to be kept warm. She debated what to do. She looked at Coop. Despite his being lanky, she couldn't lift him up and over the saddle of her horse, and with a head injury, she shouldn't try to move him. She could ride for help, but it was a good way even to Cookie's camp. She hated to leave Coop alone for that long. He could wake up and injure himself further by trying to stand.

She looked at Cinnamon. Walking to her, she spoke quietly to the young mare while she stroked her neck. "Thank you, girl. You did a wonderful job helping me to find Coop. Now I don't want to leave him alone, so can you find your way back to Ike at the barn? He'll know that I need help, and maybe Hunter'll be back by now. He'll come for me, I just know it." Hannah hugged her neck, then removed the canteen from the saddlehorn. "Thank you, sweetheart." Then she raised her voice and spoke firmly to the horse. "Now go home. Go back to the barn." She gave the horse a light swat on the rump. "Go home, girl. Go!"

The horse nodded her head and nickered, then pranced a bit before she gave Hannah one last look and galloped toward the entrance to the box canyon. Hannah watched her fade into the snowstorm and prayed that Cinnamon would be successful.

Hannah sighed. Now she really felt alone, but of course, she wasn't. She had the injured Coop to take care of, though there wasn't much she could do.

Fortunately, Coop wore his set of leather chaps which would help keep his legs warm. His jacket was open over a flannel shirt and what looked like thermal underwear. She hoped he had that on at the bottom too, though she wasn't going to look. She snapped up his jacket over his chest. He had on leather workgloves. She looked again for his hat but didn't find it.

Worried about the missing hat, she remembered that a body loses most of its heat through the top of the head. She made a quick decision, but looked around first. *Silly! No one's here but Coop, and he's unconscious.*

Moving fast, she stripped off her denim jacket and her shirt. She pulled her white T-shirt over her head and quickly replaced her shirt and jacket, shivering all the while. Kneeling beside Coop's head, she made a pad of part of the shirt and placed it under the wound, then she stretched the rest around and over his head, taking care to cover his ears and the top of his head. It wasn't much, but she hoped it would help.

Next she replaced the pine branches over him, though she allowed a little of his face to show. She took a swallow of her water, thought of giving Coop some, but knew she should wait until he was awake. She fervently hoped that would be soon.

Hannah turned her jacket collar up, pulled down her hat, and sat on the pine needles with her back against the tree. The snow had accumulated to two or three inches on the floor of the box canyon, she guessed, but under the shelter of the large pine tree there was only a light covering. She sat with one eye on Coop and the other on the entrance to the canyon.

She was hungry and wished she was at Cookie's cook camp eating beef stew, then remembered her pocket of supplies. She pulled out a granola bar, broke it into two pieces, and slowly ate one of them. She'd make it last. But Hunter would surely come soon.

Unbeknownst to Hannah, Hunter was much closer than she'd hoped.

His visit to Turk had included a stop at the sheriff's office. The two men Austin Pike had hired that summer had police records in Colorado under their real names. The names and identification they used now were false. This raised a question in Hunter's mind. Did Pike know about that?

Hunter and the sheriff discussed the past month of his nightly vigils. Nothing happened at night, so perhaps they moved the cattle in daylight? Daring, but maybe the men felt safe. So far, no one had questioned them at all. Perhaps they'd get careless.

The sheriff and Hunter devised a plan. From the office in Turk, Hunter phoned Chuck Carson and Andy Pringle,

Roy's son, and asked them to join him in a stakeout. A young deputy, Glenn Garlow, would come along to be an official and armed presence.

Hunter suspected that since Cookie's camp was set up at the end of the first dirt road into the Forest Service land, the rustlers could be using a similar road much higher up. It also led out to Turk Road. It was Carson's land across from the dirt road, and a lane there led into a cultivated field. The trees along the lane would hide the men, Hunter's truck, and the deputy's car, while they watched and waited.

They settled down for a long afternoon. All were glad they'd dressed warmly, as the day grew colder as the sky darkened.

"Looks like snow's coming," said Chuck Carson with a glance at the western sky.

"Yeah, radio said a few inches by nightfall," agreed Andy.

"Not too bad, but it's getting colder than I expected." Hunter mentally made the decision to bring the cattle down to the ranch tomorrow. Sometimes work had to be done, despite its being Sunday.

It was nearing one o'clock when the deputy said, "Look."

A cattle-hauling truck was coming down the hill from the east. It slowed and turned left onto the dirt road. The deputy trained binoculars on it and its driver. He noted the license number of the truck on a pad.

"Don't recognize the driver. The plates are Colorado. Let's give him a few minutes. I figure he'll drive farther in away from the road."

The men agreed with that.

The deputy continued, "Hunter was deputized by the sheriff, so he's legal with his rifle, but you two aren't. So, carry your rifles, but don't use them, unless it's in extreme self-defense."

Andy chuckled. "How 'extreme' is extreme self-defense, Glenn?"

The deputy grinned. "Just be careful, men. I don't want anyone's death on my conscience. We don't know how rough these men may get." Then, "Let's go."

Glenn started his car and eased it across Turk Road and blocked the exit of the cattle truck. He radioed the county dispatcher that a suspicious truck had entered the road. He asked for backup, relayed the license number, then left his car.

The men followed him across the road, then the four of them walked quietly up the dirt road keeping to the sides. They wanted to be able to duck behind a tree quickly, if necessary.

When they came to the first bend in the narrow road, Glenn held up his hand. He alone, proceeding cautiously, moved ahead through the trees.

The driver finished turning the truck in a wider place in the road and got out for a stretch. Glenn observed him checking his wristwatch, then he got back in the truck cab, pulled his ball cap over his eyes and dozed off.

Glenn slipped back to the waiting men.

"He's about five hundred yards ahead. He's turned the truck so he's headed out. Looks like he's done it before in that same spot. He checked the time, so he appears to be waiting. He looked like he was going to take a nap."

Chuck Carson said, "Dang it, Hunter, you were right! They've been operating out of the Big G all along."

"What's the plan, Glenn?" Hunter asked.

"I'm for letting him sleep. We'll let him and the others load the cattle for us, no danger of stampede if anyone uses a gun that way."

Hunter liked that idea. "I can drive them back to the ranch then and unload them. Save a lot of effort." He grinned. While he disliked knowing Austin Pike and the two hands were involved in rustling, he was glad it was about to end. He figured Chuck and Andy and the other ranchers in the area would breathe a sigh of relief too.

The deputy directed the men to take up positions surrounding the truck. Each man made sure he was well-hidden by trees, rocks or brush.

Hunter hunkered behind the thick trunk of a tree and checked the time. It was nearing 1:30. The snow hadn't started yet, though the wind had picked up. Maybe it would miss them this time, as storms had done in the past. He still wondered if Pike would be with the two hands. Somehow, he thought so, considering what Coop had said about the differing cattle counts. Hunter settled down to watch and wait.

Still sitting with her back against the big pine tree and close beside Coop, Hannah berated herself for not dressing warmer that morning. Of course, she hadn't planned to be out this long. If she hadn't discovered the men with the cattle, she'd be back in her warm log house and Cinnamon would be snug in her stall. But she was glad she'd found Coop.

She looked at him again. No change. *I wish he'd wake up!* She worried that the longer he remained unconscious, the more serious the injury to his head.

Hannah ate the other piece of her granola bar and swallowed more water. She shivered again and pulled her knees up to her chest in an effort to hold in her body heat and keep her teeth from chattering.

Her mind wandered. She vowed to buy thermal underwear like Coop's the first chance she got. Maybe even one of those sturdy rancher's jackets she'd seen Hunter wear. Surely, they came in women's sizes. They looked like they'd be very warm, practically windproof and waterproof, and they reached down over the hips. *Boy, do I wish I had one of them on now!*

Hannah knew that moving around could keep her

warmer, so she got stiffly to her feet. She leaned a hand on the tree trunk as she flexed her ankles and knees, then she circled the tree ten times, counting as she walked. She could stand upright nearer the trunk, but the long branches of the pine dipped nearly to the ground farther out. That was good, as it sheltered the small space she and Coop occupied. She knew it helped keep out some of the wind and snow.

Now Hannah sensed she had another problem. It was hours since she'd used the bathroom back at her house. She tried to ignore it but soon gave in to the pressure, besides Coop would never know. She put the tree trunk between them and walked to the far edge of the low branches. She giggled as she thought of her Grandma Withers. She'd get a chuckle out of this, as she'd always kidded Hannah about being overly modest as a girl. But it wasn't modesty that made Hannah hurry; it was the cold air.

After checking Coop to be sure he was still breathing, Hannah sat down under the tree again. She wondered if Hunter was back from Turk yet. Looking at her wristwatch, she figured Cinnamon could be back at the ranch by now, if nothing had happened to delay her. She hoped she hadn't run into trouble. Surely, Hunter would be along soon.

Hunter and the other men had been in place for about half an hour when the first snowflakes fluttered down on them. They held their places, turning up their collars and tugging down their broad-brimmed hats against the dampness.

The truck driver remained asleep. He obviously waited for his cohorts to arrive with the stolen cattle. This wasn't the first time he'd parked in that spot, Hunter felt sure. Anger simmered in him when he thought of the losses his neighbors had sustained at the hands of these lawbreakers. It galled him to know that some of his own cowhands had betrayed his trust.

The boss of the Big G silently raged against that fact for a few minutes before he set it aside as a waste of his energy.

He periodically glanced at Glenn to stay aware of any change of plan. This time, Glenn nodded and cupped a hand behind his left ear. Hunter returned the nod and listened intently. Though muffled by the few inches of snow now on the trail, he caught the sounds Glenn must have heard. The bawl of cattle and the drivers' voices as they urged them along. Hunter ventured a glance at Andy and Chuck, both of whom were alert and watching the trail.

In another few minutes, the first cows came into view. The watchers stood their ground, as planned, while the driver roused from his nap and got out of the truck. He moved to the back, unlatched the tailgate, and lowered a ramp. The skinny cowhand and the mustachioed one, still on horseback, each took a side of the ramp and prodded the cattle into the truck. Pike brought up the rear, leading Coop's horse.

Chapter Eleven

Hunter's blood froze when he saw Coop's horse. Why did Pike have it? Where was Coop? Had something happened to him? Only with supreme willpower did Hunter remain in his hiding place. He knew he had to wait until all the cattle had been loaded into the truck, per the deputy's plan. They were his cattle, but the deputy was in charge.

The truck driver complained, "What took you so long? I've been waiting almost an hour. I don't like hanging around here for that long a time."

Pike snapped back. "We're here now, ain't we? Quit complaining. You're getting your share of the money."

"The kids hung us up for awhile. Didn't go back to cook camp as soon as we expected," said Skinny.

Pike shot him a dirty look. "Keep your mouth shut." He dismounted, then led Coop's horse to the ramp and into the back of the truck. "Take this horse and sell it, the rigging too."

Jack looked questioningly at him. "Hey, I'm just selling cattle. I don't know if my contact will take a horse."

"Well, get rid of it somewhere, Jack," Pike retorted.

Carney looked around nervously. "Hurry up. I want to get back to the herd, and I'm hungry!"

140

Hunter had heard enough. He was itching to confront the thieves, and he looked toward Glenn for the go ahead. Glenn nodded, caught the eye of the other waiting ranchers, and stood.

The others followed and each left their hiding place and walked forward, their rifles trained on the rustlers.

"Freeze. You're under arrest," Glenn said in an authoritative voice.

The four culprits started to resist. Jack, spewing expletives, ran toward the driver's door of the truck. Pike ran for his horse. Skinny reached for his rifle, but Carney quickly decided to put up his hands.

Chuck Carson stopped Jack before he could get into the cab. "Hold it, mister!" He jabbed the business end of his rifle into the man's ribs.

The deputy trained his rifle on Skinny at very close range, and the man decided to let go of his own riflebutt, though he cursed all the while. "Off the horse," Glenn ordered, and Skinny complied.

While Andy held his rifle on Carney, Hunter dropped his and made a running dive for Pike. His tackle brought the man down, but he scrambled to get away. His adrenalin pumping, Hunter took great pleasure in landing a blow to his traitorous foreman's jaw.

Glenn left Chuck guarding the others while Andy loaded the rustlers' horses into the truck. He approached Pike and Hunter, who were still struggling in the snow.

"Give it up, Pike. We've got you dead to rights, and you know it." He handed Hunter his rifle, then produced a set of handcuffs and manacled the unhappy Pike.

Hunter wasn't satisfied. "Where's Coop? Why were you trying to get rid of his horse? If you've hurt that boy, I swear . . ."

Pike protested loudly. "I don't know where he is. The dumb kid must have lost his horse. We found it wandering around down the trail, and I figured to get a bit of money for it, that's all."

He cast a sullen look at Hunter and Glenn. Hunter didn't buy his story.

"You're lying, Pike. Coop would never *lose* his horse. What did you do to him?" He grabbed the man's jacket front in one hand and shook him.

Glenn said calmly, "We'll get to the bottom of this, Hunter. I'm going to call in my backup." He took his rifle back from the angry rancher, then fired one shot into the air.

In a few minutes, three more men from the sheriff's department came running. They put the others in cuffs and led them away, after a quick consultation with Glenn.

The deputy walked back to where Hunter stood. "I agree with you, Hunter. Pike's not telling us the whole truth. We'll grill him and the others. One of them was pretty nervous. Maybe he'll talk. In the meantime, I want to thank you all for your help."

Hunter brushed snow off his clothes and hat, then replaced it. "I've got to get the boys together and look for Coop, just in case he's hurt."

"I can get some help for you, if you want," Glenn offered.

"Andy and I will gladly help," Chuck said. He looked at his friend and neighbor who nodded in agreement.

"Thanks, but I think I'll get my horse and ride out to the herd. Travis or Trace may already have an idea where he could be."

"Okay. Call the office if you change your mind. We'll be in touch about the prisoners." Glenn gave them a casual salute and a grin. "I'm heading back to Turk. Want to be in on our friends' interrogation." He trod through the lightly falling snow toward his waiting car.

"Say, Hunter," Chuck began, "Andy and I'll take the cattle truck back to your place and unload them in your barnlot. You go on in the pickup."

Andy added, "We'll make a count of the cows, too, for the record then I'll call Dad to give us a lift home."

"Thanks, guys, that'll work." He picked up his rifle and started down the snowy road that Glenn had just taken. "I'll call if we need any help finding Coop. So long."

Cinnamon was an intelligent animal. Her rider had said, "Go home." Home to the horse was the warm, snug stall in the barn. She knew the way.

The cattle in Willow Valley were clustered in groups, standing with their heads together, or they were sheltered in the willows. A few bawled at the horse as she trotted by. The two young cowboys off on the other side of the valley didn't see her in the falling snow, and the snow on the ground muffled her hoofbeats.

Later, when Cinnamon reached the cook camp, she paused to drink from the stream, then went on. Inside the camper on the back of his pickup, Cookie roused from a nap on his cot. He'd gone inside to shelter himself from the storm after covering his cooking area with tarps. He checked to see if it was Hannah coming back through or the three older cowboys coming in for a meal. He was also concerned that Coop hadn't been in to eat. By the time he got outside, the horse was out of sight, leaving Cookie to wonder what had awakened him.

Cinnamon cleared the steep path that led down to the rangeland and found the gate already open. But when she came to the next pasture gate, it was latched.

The horse could jump it, but she also had seen it opened and closed many times. So using her teeth, the horse simply lifted the loop of leather strap that encircled the post and let it drop. The gate swung slightly, and the horse nudged it open and walked through. She did the same at the last gate and was soon trotting in the direction of the ranch buildings.

* * *

Hunter drove back to the Big G a bit faster than he should have considering the deteriorating road conditions. He told himself that Coop was probably just fine, holed up out of the snow somewhere, but a part of him didn't believe it. *Coop is too good a cowhand to let his horse get away from him. I'm sure Pike and the others have something to do with it.*

He parked near the horse barn and hurried inside. Ike came out of the tackroom, a concerned look on his face.

"Thank goodness, you're back, boy!"

"Things are happening, Ike. Deputy Garlow, Andy Pringle, Chuck Carson and I staked out the upper dirt road that leads into our leased land. Along about one o'clock, an empty cattle truck turned onto the road. We followed it and waited. Sometime after the snow started, Pike, Carney and Skinny showed up trailing some cattle. We caught them in the act. Chuck and Andy are behind me with the load of cattle. Pike and the others are on their way to the county jail."

As he talked, Hunter took his saddle and gear from the tackroom and walked toward The General's stall.

"Well, I'll be danged! Pike and our own hands. Who would've called that one." He stopped and looked anxiously at Hunter. "Did you see Hannah's car up at the house?"

His boss nodded. "Is she inside with Mom?"

"No. I wish she was. Hannah came over this morning. Wanted to exercise Cinnamon. Said she was only going as far as the falls and would be back in a few hours, but she's way overdue."

Hunter felt his heart jump. Hannah was up in the rough country right now? Alone?

"I hope she . . . Ike, I've got to saddle The General quick. Coop may be missing, too. You see, Pike had his horse with them and wanted their cohort at the truck to take it with the cattle and sell it. He said they just ran across it wandering back on the trail, but I don't believe him. I'm going up to the herd to check with the other boys to see if they've seen Coop." His face paled. "Now, Hannah too."

Ike said, "Here," and reached for the saddle. "I'll take care of The General, boy. You run and fetch some blankets and such, then get on up there."

The kind-hearted man was mentally berating himself for letting Hannah take Cinnamon out alone that morning.

He had the horse ready by the time Hunter returned with several blankets, his cell phone, a canteen of water, and a thermos of hot coffee provided by Elizabeth. She'd also handed him a plastic bag in which she'd quickly stuffed clean white cloths suitable for bandages. She prayed they wouldn't be needed.

The snow had let up, but Hannah felt the air was colder than before. She shivered, crossed her arms over her chest, and tucked her gloved hands under her upper arms as she paced around the tree trunk. She'd worn a path over the last few hours.

She paused beside Coop's inert form and knelt down. She brushed some snow from his cheek and wished, for the hundredth time, that he'd wake up. *Please, Lord, Coop's a fine young man. Don't let his injuries be too severe.*

Hannah started when Coop's eyelids fluttered briefly, then closed again. "Coop?" she said. "Can you hear me, Coop? It's Hannah Morgan."

She took one of his gloved hands in both hers and rubbed it, trying to warm it. She continued to talk, thinking that would help rouse him. She hoped he wouldn't fall back into unconsciousness.

"Coop? I found you here a couple hours ago. I think Pike and his men did this to you. You probably caught them with the stolen cattle. Am I right?" She bent low over him when she saw his lips move.

"What is it? What are you saying, Coop?"

"Ms. Morgan?" he whispered.

"Yes, it's me. Hannah Morgan. I'm staying with you here under this big old pine tree. It's been snowing, but we're sort of sheltered here." Hannah paused and bit her lower lip as tears welled in her eyes. "Oh, Coop, I'm so glad you're awake. I've been praying and praying for that."

She heard a weak "Thirsty . . ."

"Just a moment. I've got water." She reached for it, removed the cap, and tipped the canteen to his lips. "I'm not sure if we can do this." She was pleased that he managed to swallow twice.

He tried to lift his head for more but groaned in pain.

"Don't try to move, please. You've got a bump on the back of your head that's bled some." She didn't tell him that it'd bled a lot. "I wrapped your head to cover the cut and to help keep you warm. Do you hurt anywhere else?"

He didn't reply at first, then said, "Leg."

"Yes, your right leg looks broken, I'm afraid. That's another reason to just lie still. There'll be help coming soon." She hoped desperately that she wasn't lying.

"Pike . . . cattle."

"Yes, Coop, I know. I saw him, but he didn't see me. I even took some pictures, and I heard enough to know that you were hurt and lying somewhere. Cinnamon and I rode all over this box canyon before we finally found you."

Hannah reached into her jacket pocket and produced a chocolate bar. Breaking off a tiny square, she offered it to Coop.

"Are you hungry? I've eaten a granola bar, but maybe you could let this chocolate just dissolve on your tongue?"

Coop opened his eyes again. She was gratified to see that they could focus on her face. "Thanks."

"You're welcome," she replied and grinned widely in relief. She placed the candy on his tongue.

After a few moments of savoring the chocolate, he asked, "Where's the boss?"

"He went to Turk this morning, but I hope he's back by now. I sent Cinnamon back to the barn. She seemed to understand what I wanted and took off at a gallop. I told her to find Ike and Hunter and bring them here. I just hope she got to the barn okay."

"She's smart. She'll get there," Coop whispered.

"Then they'll be here soon, and we'll get you out of here and to the clinic in Turk. It'll be okay."

As he led The General to the barn door, Hunter said to Ike, "When I find them, Coop may be hurt. I'm praying Hannah isn't, but—anyway, I'll use the cell phone to call 911, but if the signal can't get over the mountains to them, I'll try you down here."

Ike nodded. "I'll stay by the phone, ready to relay any info you have. Now, be on your way, Hunter, and good luck."

Hunter nodded, his face grim, and he and his horse stepped through the sliding door. He mounted and urged The General forward, intent on catching up with the young cowhands in Willow Valley.

He reined in abruptly when he heard muffled hoofbeats coming toward him around the corral. His hope that it was Hannah faded quickly. "Ike!" he shouted, and the older man came outside. "It's Cinnamon," he said in alarm, "but no rider."

The two men exchanged a worried look.

"Cinnamon wouldn't throw Hannah. She's a good rider, and she and the horse get along fine," Ike offered.

"That's true enough, but where is she?"

Ike heard the deep concern in Hunter's voice.

The horse had stopped a few feet from The General. She pawed the snowy ground and snorted great puffs of hot breath into the cold air. Then, she turned back the way she'd come and pranced a few steps. She moved back to Hunter, then repeated the motion.

"Look at Cinnamon, boy."

"She knows where Hannah is," Hunter almost shouted. "She wants to lead me there. Come on, boy," he said to The General, "let's go."

Cinnamon took off at a run with The General close behind her. Hunter's trusted horse needed no more urging to follow.

They made good time, despite the snowy condition of the rangeland, as Cinnamon retraced her own hoofprints. Hunter was surprised at the gates being open. He felt that Hannah would have closed them behind her earlier in the day, but perhaps she'd been distracted.

They were soon at the cook camp. The horses paused to drink from the stream, while Hunter shouted for Cookie.

The door to the camper shell opened and the man stuck his head out. "That you, Hunter?"

He gave the surprised cook a succinct version of what had happened and of his concern for Coop and Hannah.

"Cinnamon's leading me to Hannah. I hope we can find Coop, too, before nightfall."

Having drunk their fill, the horses were ready to move again.

"Good luck, boss. Be careful too," he called as horse and rider disappeared up the trail behind Cinnamon.

When they gained Willow Valley, Hunter looked around for the boys. He saw Trace near the creek and shouted to him.

"Trace, get Travis and follow me. The herd will stay put in this snow. We've got to find Coop and Hannah. Coop's likely hurt. I hope that she isn't too." He rode on.

Trace waved to Travis, who by now had noticed his boss across the expanse of the valley.

Travis crossed to his brother. "What's up?"

"Hunter said to come with him. He thinks Coop's lying hurt somewhere. Maybe Ms. Morgan too." He started in the direction his boss had ridden.

"Hurt? Dang, that must be why he didn't come in for a meal," Travis surmised as he and his mount fell into step beside Trace.

"We haven't seen Pike and the others either. I wonder if they've got something to do with this?" Trace said soberly.

Travis agreed. "We've been suspicious of them for awhile, especially Coop. Maybe Coop caught them at something?"

"Likely. Hunter looked real worried."

The two Jeromes picked up speed as they followed the tracks in the snow.

By this time, Hunter had reached the end of the valley. He wasn't surprised that Cinnamon made straight for the path that led up toward the waterfall. That was the way Hannah and he always took on their Sunday afternoon rides, and Ike had said she planned to ride to the waterfall.

He had a sudden chilling thought. A vision of Hannah falling into the water. "No!" he muttered, "surely not." She was a careful person. But his thoughts grew darker when he realized she could have slipped on the snow and tumbled. "Please, Lord, let her be safe. I—she means a lot to me. And let Coop be all right." He mentally chastised himself for momentarily forgetting Coop.

He gained the waterfall area. To Hunter's relief, Cinnamon didn't slacken her pace but continued on her way.

"Good," he breathed. Cinnamon obviously hadn't left Hannah at the waterfall.

A short time later, they reached the three springs. That was the farthest Hannah and he ever rode together, so he was very surprised when Cinnamon passed them by and crossed the narrow stream that the springs formed.

Why would she ride farther on her own? She didn't know the trails up ahead. Did she get lost? If she had, Cinnamon would have found the way back for her. His stomach tightened as he thought again of what the horse's solitary return to the barn might mean—Hannah alone and hurt somewhere up here. There were so many washes and coulees, so many little canyons and draws. *How will I find her?* He briefly felt panic set in before he sternly reminded himself of Cinnamon's ability.

"Trust the horse, man. She knows where she's headed. I hope it's straight to Hannah."

Hunter heard the boys behind him on the trail, and he paused to let them catch up. Cinnamon was looking for the way down into a steep-sided ravine just ahead.

In a terse tone, he told them quickly that Cinnamon had returned to the barn without her rider and of the arrest of Pike, Skinny, and Carney for rustling.

"Pike said they'd found Coop's horse just wandering, but I don't believe that for a minute. I think they've hurt him and left him on his own. I just hope he's alive when we find him."

"Dang! We should've looked for Coop sooner. We couldn't figure out why he didn't come in to eat." Travis slapped his right thigh in self-disgust.

"Yeah," his brother agreed, "but how did Ms. Morgan get mixed up in this? We haven't seen her today."

"I don't know, boys. Ike said she asked to take Cinnamon out for a ride to the waterfall this morning and was overdue, then Cinnamon came galloping up to me when I was starting off to look for Coop." Hunter, who had been watching the horse, added, "There she goes, boys. Follow me."

It was a slow process, but Cinnamon carefully picked her way down into the coulee, then she crossed it unerringly to the narrow entrance to the box canyon. She paused and turned to the others as they rode toward her. When they reached her, she trotted through the opening.

Coop ate another bite of chocolate, and Hannah helped him with the water canteen for another few swallows. She sipped a little herself before she replaced the cap.

She began to rise to stretch her legs again when she caught the high nicker of a horse. Coop heard it as well.

"Stay down," he warned.

Hannah did so, but peeked through the low branches toward the opening to the canyon. Did Coop think it was Pike and his men back to check on him? See if he was still alive? A tremor ran through her at that possibility. Coop and she were defenseless.

But it could also be Cinnamon. She hoped and prayed that it was, and with Hunter too. She closed her eyes. *Please, Lord, let it be Hunter.*

Hannah took a deep breath and opened her eyes. There was a horse just emerging from the narrow entrance. It was Cinnamon.

"Coop, it's Cinnamon! She's come back," she whispered.

Coop's body tensed. "Is—is anyone with her?"

Hannah grabbed his hand in reassurance and waited. Then, she saw a beautiful sight. A big gray horse with a rider on his back who could only be Hunter.

"Yes, Coop," she answered excitedly. "It's Hunter on The General and—and Travis and Trace are behind him. Thank God, Coop, they've come. Cinnamon did it; she led them to us."

Coop's hand trembled in hers. "Thank you, too, Ms. Morgan."

Hannah smiled, leaned down and kissed his cold cheek.

"I'll be right back." She got up, ducked under the pine branches and waved her right arm over her head. She saw Cinnamon trotting toward her with The General at a gallop passing her by. He kicked up a shower of snow as his rider reined him in a few yards from where she stood waiting.

Hannah's gratitude at seeing Hunter showed on her face, as he leaped off his horse and covered the space between them. He swept her into his arms and hugged her tightly.

She had never felt so secure and happy. "Oh, Hunter, I knew you'd come."

"Are you all right, Hannah? Are you injured? Pike and his men didn't hurt you?" He set her away from him, but with his hands still on her shoulders, studied her face and looked over the length of her.

"I'm fine really, just cold and hungry. But Coop's here with me, and he needs medical help."

Hunter reached for the blankets tied behind his saddle and draped one around her, then grabbed the thermos of coffee from a saddlebag.

She led the way as Hunter and the cowhands crowded into the space under the big pine tree.

"Hi," Coop said shyly.

"Hi, yourself, Coop," Travis replied, his relief at Coop's being alive apparent in his voice. He and Trace hunkered down on the far side of Coop's inert form. Hunter and Hannah did the same on his left.

"Pike did this, Coop?" he asked although he felt sure he already knew.

"Yeah. I'm sorry, boss, but they got away with some cattle they had hidden up here. I tried to . . ."

"I know, Coop. Thanks for trying, but you should've gotten the rest of us to help instead of taking such a chance. You could've been . . ." Hunter's voice choked. "Anyway, they didn't get away with it. The cattle are safe at the ranch, and Pike and the others are in jail."

Coop grinned in relief, as did Hannah.

"Thank goodness!" she exclaimed and accepted the thermos lid full of still hot coffee Trace had poured for her. The warmth felt wonderful as she sipped it slowly.

"I want to hear all the details of what happened up here," Hunter said, "but much later after we get some help for you. Where are you hurt?"

Hannah described Coop's injuries, and Hunter went to his saddlebags to retrieve the cell phone. Travis and Trace removed the pine branches covering Coop and carefully tucked two blankets over him.

Hunter returned. "I couldn't get through to Turk, but I got Ike down at the ranch. He's calling for the emergency guys to come out. I told him to tell them one of us would meet them at the end of the access road so they won't miss the turn, then we can guide them back in here."

"I'll go," Travis got up to leave.

"Thanks for coming, you guys," Coop said.

"Yes, thank you very much," added Hannah. "We were afraid for a few minutes that it was Pike and his men coming back."

"Had they seen you, Hannah?" Hunter asked with a frown on his forehead.

"No. I'd ridden up to the waterfall to take pictures and be alone for awhile." She ducked her head over her coffee for a moment, then looked back at him. "Anyway, I decided I wanted a few shots of the three springs, so Cinnamon and I rode on up there. She heard a sound and after a minute, I did too. I couldn't quite identify it, so we crossed the little stream and rode toward the sound."

Hunter let out an exasperated snort. "Hannah, you'd never ridden past the springs before. Didn't you think you could be riding into danger?"

"Well, that's true, but Cinnamon knew her way around, and Ike and Cookie knew where I was headed," she said in self-defense. "Besides, there was no one in Willow Valley when I rode through. I figured the cowboys had gone in for a meal and that I was alone up here." She paused to sip her warming drink. "As we got closer I recognized the sound of cattle bawling and moving around. I'll admit that I was startled when I heard a voice yelling at the cattle, but then I supposed that was why the guys hadn't been with the herd. They were up here rounding up strays."

Hunter shifted on the ground. "I'll agree, that would be the logical conclusion." He still looked irritated, which Hannah noted.

"I wanted to get some pictures of that, so I tied Cinnamon to a tree and got closer to the side of the coulee out there. It dropped off steeply so I kept some big rocks between me and the edge. I was glad I had when I saw Skinny and Carney with some cattle down below me. The younger guys were nowhere around, and I don't feel comfortable with Pike and the others, but I snapped a few shots of them and the cows."

Hunter perked up. "You did? That may be useful when they go to trial."

Hannah smiled. She felt off the hook in some odd way.

"Yes, they could be. In fact, it's the type of film that has the date and time printed on the photos. My camera's still in Cinnamon's saddlebag."

"You said they didn't see you. What happened next?" Trace asked from the other side of Coop. He and the injured cowboy had been listening.

Hannah briefly told them of seeing Pike hide the metal gate that had blocked the entrance to the box canyon and of their conversation.

"I was really worried when I recognized your horse, Coop. Pike took him with him when he left."

She paused and looked imploringly at Hunter.

Hunter nodded and got up. He held out a hand to her. She set her empty cup on the ground and allowed him to pull her to her feet.

"Let's walk for a bit," he suggested.

"Okay." She pulled the blanket snug around her, and they ducked under the branches.

Chapter Twelve

The General and Cinnamon saw them and walked forward, so Hannah and Hunter met the horses away from the tree. Hannah hugged Cinnamon around the neck and thanked her for saving them. The horse nodded, tossed her head, and nickered loudly.

"She's wonderful, Hunter. I told her I needed your help and to go home to the barn and get you or Ike and bring you back here. She seemed to understand perfectly and took off at a run. By that time it'd gotten colder and was snowing."

Hunter patted the horse's neck and praised her as well. Then, not to exclude The General, both Hannah and he fussed over him.

"Was there something you didn't want to say in front of Coop?" he prompted.

"Carney asked Pike if he'd 'hid him good', and Pike answered that no one would find him until they were long gone from here. Skinny said he hated to see them lose this sweet little set-up, or something like that. Carney seemed really nervous and wanted to get going. It wasn't until they drove the cattle up the trail and Pike led away the horse that I recognized it as the one Coop always rides. Then I knew they'd been talking about him. I debated what to do, then decided I should waste no time finding Coop. Pike had implied that he was dead, and I was afraid I'd find him that way. But, if he wasn't already, he could be by the time I'd found help."

Hannah suddenly shivered and clutched her blanket closer.

"You're still cold. Let's get back under the tree. It's more sheltered from the wind there." He slipped an arm about her shoulders and walked her to the tree. Under the branches, he poured another cup from the thermos and sat down with his back to the tree trunk in the clear spot Hannah had used. "Sit with me, Hannah. We need to warm you up."

She began to sit beside him, but he surprised her. He took her hand in his free one and tugged her gently onto his lap.

"Hunter, I don't think . . ."

"Don't be foolish, Hannah. Trace and Coop don't mind, do you?"

Trace flashed a quick grin. "Gosh, no, boss."

"Here, take your coffee. It's still warm, and you need that."

When both hands were free, he tucked her blanket around her and pulled her close.

Hannah sipped her coffee and shivered again, but soon she felt less chilled. The coffee and the blanket combined with the warmth of Hunter's arms did their work well.

"Thank you. I feel much better now."

"Good," he said quietly and rested his cheek on the top of her head for just a moment, but she was aware of it. She blinked to stop sudden hot tears and swallowed hard.

"I'm still upset with you, Hannah, for going off past the springs alone, but I'm proud of you too. You're very brave."

She silently shook her head in denial.

"Yes, you are!" he said insistently, though in a low voice, his lips near her ear. "Coop may owe his life to you. His wounds may not be life-threatening, but without your help we may not have found him in time. Between tonight's cold temperatures and his not being able to move, well, you know what I mean."

Hannah dashed a tear away with a gloved finger. "I was so afraid that he was already dead when I finally found him under this tree. Those horrible men! Hunter, they'd— they'd left him for *dead!* He had a heartbeat, but he was unconscious for such a long time. I prayed and prayed."

"I did that myself while I was following Cinnamon up here. I was so afraid for you and Coop."

"I'm sorry that I worried you, Hunter, but I'll be okay now, and Coop will be when he has medical care."

Feeling very tired, Hannah set her empty cup on a bare patch of pine needles and closed her eyes, her left cheek resting on Hunter's chest.

Hunter gently eased her cowgirl hat into a tilt so the brim wouldn't be crushed while she slept. He watched her face. Her dark-brown eyelashes fluttered once, and her lips parted slightly as she made a small sound. He thought she must be dreaming.

He mentally gave thanks for her safety and for young Coop's surviving his ordeal. The boy was smart and good-natured, and he had good cow and horse sense. Once he was well, Hunter considered offering the foreman's job to him. He may be young, but he instinctively knew he could trust him. He decided to give it more thought when things settled down.

Hunter laid his head back against the tree. Pike had come with good references when he hired on at the Big G Cattle Company more than a year ago. Hunter had checked them out himself. He wondered where Pike had gone wrong.

He looked again at Hannah's sleeping face. It felt wonderful to hold her close. They'd become such good friends in a short time. The thought of her leaving after the school year ended pained him. He decided to give *her* more thought, too, when things settled down.

He roused himself from those thoughts when he heard a call from the entrance to the canyon. He patted Hannah's shoulder. "Wake up, Hannah. The boys are back with the emergency squad."

She sat up straight and slid off his lap, looking somewhat confused.

"Just stay put here now. Lean against the tree. When they have Coop on his way, we'll ride Cinnamon and The General back to the ranch. A warm bath and supper sound good, don't they?" He smiled down at her.

She smiled in return. She felt nicely warmed now, content to sit under the tree and let the others take care of the injured cowboy.

Twenty minutes later, the two emergency workers had given Coop an injection to lessen the pain that moving him would cause, then put a splint on his broken leg before carefully lifting him onto a stretcher. They carried him out of the canyon to the ambulance that they had parked at the top of the rise out of the coulee. Though it was equipped with four-wheel drive, they felt it best to walk part of the way.

Hunter didn't let Coop go without knowing that all his medical expenses would be covered and that he'd be in later that evening to see him.

The Jerome boys started back to the herd, but Hunter stopped them. "It's going to be cold tonight, fellows. See that the herd's bedded down for the night, then come on in to the bunkhouse. You can come back up and check the cows tomorrow, and we'll trail them down to the ranch in a few days. I'll have Cookie break camp too."

"Thanks, boss," Travis said with a grin. "I'm looking forward to sleeping in my own warm bed."

"Me too," his brother added, "and we don't have to worry about rustlers anymore."

Hunter laughed. "That sure puts *my* mind at ease. See you later."

The cowhands rode out of the canyon.

He called his horse and Cinnamon as he turned back to the tree. He found Hannah sitting in the same place.

"Is Coop doing okay?" she asked as she began to get to her feet. Hunter took her arm and helped her.

"They'll take good care of him. I'll drive in to Turk later to see what the doctor says." He smiled warmly at her. "Are you ready to ride?"

Hannah nodded and looked around. She picked up the thermos lid and Hunter got the thermos and screwed the lid in place. She found her canteen and said, "Now I am."

"I see you remembered what I told you that first day we rode out together." He gestured toward the canteen.

"Well, sort of," she admitted sheepishly. "Ike gave me this when I asked to take Cinnamon out." She walked to her horse and hung the canteen over the saddlehorn. "But, I remembered to put a granola bar in my pocket. I ate it earlier while Coop was still unconscious, but I fed him a little chocolate later on and sips of water."

Hunter stowed the thermos in a saddlebag, rolled the blankets, and tied them behind his saddle before he turned back to her.

"That probably helped keep him warm while you waited."

Hannah reached into her jacket pocket and removed the remainder of the chocolate bar.

"It's a bit squashed, but would you like to share the rest?"

Hunter grinned. "Sounds good. I missed lunch too." He took the squares she offered and ate them. She did the same with hers.

Hannah thought he had an odd look on his face.

"Is something wrong?"

"No, at least I don't think so." He stepped nearer her and looked into her eyes. They widened as she realized his intention, but she didn't back away. "Hannah?"

She gave no reply, simply lifted her arms and face to him as he tipped back his hat and lowered his mouth to hers. It wasn't a very long kiss, nor demanding—just gentle and loving. Hannah sighed when their lips parted.

Hunter hugged her for a moment, then stated, "You taste like chocolate."

Hannah giggled. "You do too!"

Hunter's arms tightened about her. "I really like chocolate."

"Me too," she managed to say before he added a second kiss.

They looked at one another and smiled. Something had happened there, but neither of them wanted to try to put a name on it. Not just yet, anyway.

They mounted the patiently waiting horses. Hannah looked around the box canyon once more before she and Cinnamon started forward.

"This is a lovely place, Hunter. To think, I may never have gotten to see it, if I hadn't accidentally come across the rustlers."

"That's true, and it is a pretty spot. We'll have to ride up here again one day."

They exchanged a smile, and Hunter reached across the space between Cinnamon and The General and squeezed her hand.

When they reached the cook camp, they found the cowboys there already. They had filled Cookie in on as much as they knew of the afternoon's events. Now they helped him pack up supplies and equipment to be hauled back to the ranch.

"We're going on to the house. Hannah needs to get really warmed before she catches a cold or something," Hunter explained. "I'm driving to Turk to check on Coop later. I'll stop by the bunkhouse after I'm back. See you then."

"Take good care of her now, Hunter, and we'll be waiting to hear from you."

Hunter glanced over his shoulder at his employees who were grinning broadly at Hannah and him. "Yes, Cookie," he said meekly, then laughed aloud.

Hannah waved as they rode away.

"I could be wrong, but I think our boss has found himself a right fine young woman there," Cookie exclaimed.

"That's the way Trace and I are readin' it," Travis said.

"Yep," his brother agreed.

Hunter used the cell phone to contact Ike at the tackroom. He told him that Hannah and he would be in soon, followed by the boys and Cookie. They were packing it in up here.

It was completely dark when Ike greeted them at the barn door. He'd been watching anxiously for them.

They dismounted and led the horses inside to their stalls. Hannah meant to rub Cinnamon down, but Ike said, "Now let me do that this time. You go on to the house. Elizabeth is worried about the two of you. I'll tend to The General too, Hunter."

"Thanks, Ike," Hunter replied.

Hannah gave the old man a hug. "Thank you," she murmured before she let Hunter take her hand and lead her toward the door. "Goodnight, Cinnamon dear." The horse responded with a toss of her head and a soft nicker.

Ike turned to his task. He removed the horse's saddle and blanket, then said, "You and Hannah get along right fine, don't you? I think you even understand her words." He patted her back and began rubbing her down with a warmed rag.

Up at the house, Elizabeth was overjoyed to see them back. She hugged them both, then helped Hannah out of her jacket and hung it and her hat on pegs on the backporch with Hunter's.

"I know you're anxious to hear all that happened, Mom, but Hannah got really chilled up there. Can you run her a warm bath and find her something to wear?"

"Of course, son. Now come upstairs, and we'll get right to that." She slipped an arm around Hannah's waist as they walked to the stairs. "Don't want you getting sick over this, dear. Oh, the coffee's fresh, Hunter. We'll eat as soon as Hannah's ready."

Hungry, Hunter peeked into the oven wondering what his mother had prepared. He found a larger than usual meatloaf, a big pot of mashed potatoes on a back burner, a pan of simmering tomato sauce, and over on the counter a freshly-baked chocolate cake.

His mouth watered. He decided his mother must be inviting all the hands in to eat tonight. *Good.* They could talk about what'd happened today all at once, then he could go check on Coop's condition.

He took the back stairs two at a time. He intended to get some clean clothes and shower in the downstairs bathroom. He rubbed a hand over his past five o'clock shadow. His shaver was in there with Hannah. He paused, debating with himself, then rapped on the bathroom door.

"Who is it?" Definitely Hannah's voice.

"Uh, it's Hunter. I need to shave. Would you hand out my razor, please? It's on a shelf next to the sink."

Silence. "Well, okay, just a minute." Then, she muttered to herself, "Luckily, I hadn't gotten into the tub yet." She struggled into an oversized terry robe she took from a hook on the back of the door. Too late, she realized it was Hunter's, as she caught a whiff of aftershave and froze for a moment.

She grabbed the electric razor, opened the door a crack and shoved her forearm through. "Here," she said a bit tartly.

He took the razor. "Thanks."

"You're welcome." She closed the door again.

Hunter walked away toward his bedroom with a little smile playing about his lips.

A few minutes later, Hannah was soaking in a warm tub of fragrant orange blossom bubbles. They smelled heavenly. Another rap on the door startled her.

"Is that you again, Hunter?" she asked sharply without thinking. To her chagrin, his mother answered instead.

"No, dear, it's Elizabeth with a warm nightie and robe for you to put on when you're ready."

Oh no! Hannah knew her face turned red, but she tried to answer calmly. "I'm in the tub, but the door's unlocked. Please, just bring them in."

Hannah was well-hidden by the bubbles, but she still scooted down in the tub a bit. "Thank you for the clothes, Elizabeth. I'm sorry I snapped at you. Earlier, before I was in the tub, Hunter had knocked and asked for his razor. I handed it out to him. I—I guess I thought he'd come back for something else."

"Oh. Well, he generally does have to shave twice a day. My father was like that too." She smiled at the young woman, hoping to put her at ease. "This nightie may be long on you, but it's warm and not see-through. So's the robe, and here's a pair of quilted bootie slippers. I earlier told Ike to invite Cookie and the boys up to the house for supper, when he told me they were all coming in tonight. I hope you don't mind?"

"Of course not. I'm comfortable with all of them, so a warm flannel robe will be fine. Unless you want me to put my jeans back on?"

"Heavens no, dear. They're probably dirty after the day

you've had. Say, I'll run your things through the washer while we're eating. Now, I'll let you enjoy your soak." She gathered Hannah's discarded clothing and left.

Elizabeth is so very thoughtful. But Hannah still felt embarrassed by reacting to her knock the way she had.

Half an hour later, she joined Elizabeth in the kitchen. The lady smiled at her.

"You look much better, Hannah. Warmer and more relaxed. The robe and nightgown fit pretty well after all."

"I just hitched the gown up a bit with the belt of the robe. Thank you so much for loaning them to me. Supper smells wonderful!"

"Nothing fancy, but that's the way Hunter and the guys like it," Elizabeth said with a chuckle. "Now, you just go ahead and sit down at the table. Would you like a cup of tea, dear? I want to keep you warm."

"That sounds good. Thank you." Hannah saw that Elizabeth had extended the table, covered it with a bright red cloth, and set it with her white dinner service.

Hannah was steeping a tea bag in a china cup when Hunter emerged from the bathroom off the hall and joined them in the kitchen. He sat at the table across from Hannah and looked at her closely.

"How do you feel? Better, I hope. I know I do."

Hannah smiled. "Just fine, Hunter. Toasty warm again."

"Me too."

He thought that she looked beautiful with her hair brushed out, her cheeks rosy pink, and her gray eyes shining warmly at him.

His mother set a cup of coffee before him. He nodded his thanks and took a sip. He'd just had an extraordinary thought and wondered if it showed on his face for her and Hannah to see.

A rap on the back door brought him to his feet, and he called, "Come in, fellows."

Ike entered first followed by Cookie and the Jerome

brothers. Each wiped their boots on the handy boot scraper and hung hats and jackets on the pegs on the wall of the backporch. By the time all were in the kitchen and seated at the table, Elizabeth and Hannah, who had risen to help, had put the platter of sliced meat loaf and the additional dishes on the table.

Hunter waited until the ladies sat down, then asked the others to bow their heads. He expressed gratitude for their meal, the apprehension of the rustlers, and the safety of Hannah. He concluded with heart-felt concern for young Coop. His "Amen" was echoed by the others.

When all had filled their plates and begun their meal, Elizabeth asked, "Now, Hunter, I'm anxious to know what's happened today?"

"Well, there are some things that we won't know until Coop can tell us, but here's my part."

He told the group around the table about the nightly vigils he'd kept for the past month or so.

"You sure stayed out of sight," commented Travis.

"We didn't have any idea you were up there at night," added Cookie.

"Only Ike and the sheriff knew about it," he offered as his mother expressed her concern. "That's why I didn't tell you, Mom. I knew you'd worry. Anyway, I had a call from the sheriff this morning, and I drove in to talk with him. He'd finally gotten a report that showed that Carney and Skinny had prison records under their real names. I wondered if Pike knew that as he'd recommended they be hired. I blame myself for not checking personally." He frowned and chewed a bite of meat loaf.

"We decided," he continued, "if nothing was happening at night, they could be moving them a few at a time during broad daylight."

"That'd explain Coop's tallies not matching old Pike's," inserted Trace. "Pike was lying to cover up."

"Yeah," Travis agreed.

Hunter answered a few more questions, and told the group about the plan he and the sheriff had hatched and of the help from their two neighbors. They all agreed luck had been with them to catch the rustlers red-handed on their first try at a stakeout.

"Did they put up much of a fight, boss?" asked Travis eagerly. Truth be known, he and his younger brother both wished they'd been there.

"No, not much. We totally surprised them." Hunter played down his part in stopping Pike. "Anyway, they're in the county jail now."

"And good riddance," Cookie said vehemently.

Hunter looked at Hannah across the table. She looked back and was relieved when he smiled. She returned the smile, then glanced around the table. She had grown very fond of these fine people and looked upon them all as friends.

"I guess it's my turn to fill in the story. First, I'm truly sorry for causing you any worry, Ike."

She was rewarded with a big smile from the old man. "I'm just happy that you're safe and sound, young lady."

"And Hunter already has had my apology. You see, I took Cinnamon out about mid-morning." She continued with how she happened upon the rustlers, what she'd seen and heard, then her search for Coop. "When I finally found him, he wasn't moving. I was plenty scared. He had a bump on his head and a broken right leg." She concluded with praise for Cinnamon's ability to go back to the barn on her own.

"That's one smart horse," Ike said admiringly, "and one smart young woman to think of sending the horse back to the barn."

The others murmured their agreement, and Hannah blushed.

"Believe me, I just did the only things I could think of for Coop."

"I think Hannah saved Coop's life. Who knows how long it may have taken us to find him out there," Hunter concluded and pushed back his plate.

"My goodness, yes," Elizabeth added.

Cookie, his faded blue eyes suspiciously bright, inserted, "I'm real glad you and the boy made it through. I was a bit worried when Coop didn't come in for his noon meal, then later when you didn't stop at my camp on your way out. I had no idea what was happening just a few miles away."

Ike echoed Cookie's sentiments. "I know I was sure glad to see Hunter when he got back. I hated to have to tell him you were overdue on Cinnamon."

"Thanks, Ms. Morgan," said Trace quietly.

"Yeah, Ms. Morgan, we'd sure hate to lose old Coop," added his brother.

"Please, all of you, call me Hannah. I'm Ms. Morgan at school, but I'd like my friends to think of me as Hannah. I'm just glad I happened along at the right time today. But Cinnamon deserves your thanks more than I do. She saved the day for both Coop and me."

In a short while, after pieces of chocolate cake and thanks to Elizabeth for the fine meal, the men excused themselves and returned to the bunkhouse. As Hannah and Elizabeth cleared the table, Hunter prepared to leave for Turk.

He took Hannah aside. "Please stay overnight with us. I'll feel better knowing you're safe and sound here with Mom while I'm gone."

Hannah began to protest, but the concern on his face and in his voice stopped her. "Sure, Hunter, if that helps you, and if it's all right with Elizabeth."

He took one of her hands in his and turned to his mother.

"Mom, I want Hannah to stay with us tonight. Okay?"

Elizabeth couldn't miss the warmth in his tone or his holding Hannah's hand. She smiled happily.

"Of course, son. I was going to suggest it myself. Now, drive carefully." She turned back to her dishwasher.

Hunter tugged on Hannah's hand so she'd follow him onto the back porch. He slipped into his coat and reached for his hat.

"I wish you didn't have to go out again. Tell Coop I'll be in to visit him whenever the doctor allows." She patted Hunter's arm.

He grinned. "Lucky Coop."

Chapter Thirteen

Hannah smiled back, then Hunter did what he'd been wanting to do since before supper. He kissed her.

She kissed him back. It seemed like the most natural thing in the world to do right then.

"If I'm asleep when you get back, please wake me. I want to hear what the doctor says about Coop's condition." She touched the side of his face and smiled.

"You bet, Hannah. Oh, is your camera still in that saddle-bag? That film may be of interest to the sheriff."

"Yes, it is. Take it with you, please."

"Bye."

"Bye, yourself." She closed the outer door behind him. She watched until she saw the lights of the pickup come on, and he drove out the lane. She still stood there as she wondered what was happening to her. She brought her hands to her warm face and touched a fingertip to her lips.

Could Hunter have fallen in love with her? Plain, shy Hannah Morgan? The young woman who felt more at ease with her students than the adults she mingled with? But the people of the Big G and the community had welcomed her so warmly. She liked them very much. The next question

169

was had she fallen in love with Hunter? She strongly suspected she had—slowly, over time.

Hannah was startled by Elizabeth's voice calling her name, and she rejoined her in the kitchen.

Hunter's kiss must still have shown on her face, because his mother's face lit up in delight. "Oh, Hannah!" She opened her arms to the young woman who happily hugged her in return. "I'm so glad that Hunter wanted you to stay with us tonight. I must say that from the first day I met you, I hoped that you and he would hit it off."

"Thank you, Elizabeth. But . . . well, yes, he's kissed me today, but . . . but I don't really know how he feels inside. Maybe it was just relief that I'm okay, or that Coop was found, or the rustlers were caught. I just don't know."

Her few minutes of elation were being quickly replaced by old feelings of unsureness and inadequacy.

"Now, don't fret, Hannah. Hunter often does keep his thoughts to himself, but I've noticed that he likes spending time with you. He's not hiding that. So, let an old woman hope, all right?"

She smiled warmly at Hannah.

"He *is* a fine man," Hannah offered. "He's very kind and thoughtful. Very handsome too," she added with a twinkle in her eyes. "I—I like spending time with him, too."

"Good, that's a start. Now, you've had a difficult day, dear, so let me show you where to sleep when you're ready." Hannah followed her up the stairs from the kitchen.

Later, Elizabeth and she sat up in the living room waiting for Hunter's return. The older woman told her several anecdotes about the Whetstone community, her own youth and early married years, and a few humorous tales of Hunter's boyhood infractions.

Hannah enjoyed that, and she responded with some memories of her own, though she didn't talk in detail of her relationship with her sister.

Elizabeth had lit a fire in the fireplace, and now they

both were growing sleepy. Hannah stretched out on the sofa cuddled under one of Elizabeth's pretty afghans while Elizabeth put away her current knitting project, leaned back in her comfortable chair, and closed her eyes. They had both dozed for awhile when they awakened to the sound of Hunter's truck in the barnyard. He didn't come in immediately, and Hannah supposed that he had stopped at the bunkhouse to tell the men the news first, before he came into the house.

Elizabeth rose to make cups of cocoa. Hannah folded her coverlet and patted her hair smooth. She nearly laughed aloud at herself. *Why did I do that?*

A few minutes later, Hunter walked into the room in his socks, having left his wet boots on the back porch, and crossed to the sofa. Then Hannah knew why she'd done it—some small, vain part of her wanted to look nice for him.

He held out one strong hand. She took it and let him pull her to her feet. She looked up at him questioningly and was thrilled by his smile.

"Hello, Hannah," Hunter said in that voice that reminded her of warm, melting chocolate. He pulled her into his arms.

Hannah placed her hands on his chest. "I'm glad you're back, Hunter." Then her hands slipped up around his neck as he kissed her.

"What a nice welcome. A fellow could get used to this," he whispered in her ear when their lips parted.

"Mm-hm-m," she murmured in agreement, then stepped back. "You're cold, Hunter. Please, sit near the fire. Your mother and I have been enjoying it."

Elizabeth returned with a tray holding three cups.

"Cocoa, Mom? I can't remember the last time I had a cup."

She sat in her chair with her own cup. "I thought it would be a good warmer-upper."

Hannah sat back down on the sofa, near but not too near

Hunter. She sipped her hot cocoa then asked the question that was paramount: "What did the doctor say?"

"Well, the good news is there's no skull fracture. He'd lost a lot of blood from the scalp wound. I gave a pint while I was there; we're the same type. That's what took me so long. I had to wait a half hour before I could leave." He paused to drink from his cup.

"That was very good of you, Hunter," Hannah murmured.

He shook his head. "Just something to do to help Coop and the clinic. His leg is the real problem. The doctor says it'll need surgery. They'll move him to the hospital in Bozeman for that tomorrow."

"Oh, dear," Elizabeth fretted.

"He'll be fine, Mom. He's young and strong."

"Thank goodness." Hannah closed her eyes for a moment of silent prayer for the cowboy. "Does Coop remember how it happened?"

"Well, he said Pike and the others caught him in that box canyon. Pike distracted him by trying to convince him to join up with them while Skinny edged his horse in behind him. Skinny hit him with something, probably his rifle butt, on the back of the head. He must have caught a spur on a stirrup and twisted his leg when he fell off his horse. It's a really bad break. He can't remember hitting the ground."

"I thought it could have happened that way," Hannah agreed.

"Well, kids, I was asleep in my chair earlier, so I'm going to go up to bed." She rose to take her soiled cup to the kitchen. "Now Hannah, you sleep in if you want. It's Sunday, but we'll decide in the morning if we're going to church."

"Goodnight, Elizabeth," Hannah said warmly, "and thanks again for your help and . . . and everything."

"You're welcome, dear. 'Night, son."

"Goodnight."

They fell silent while they finished their cocoa and placed the cups on the tray.

Hannah suddenly felt skittish. "I'll take them to the kitchen." She rose to do that.

"Okay," Hunter agreed, "but come back, please. I'd like to talk."

In the kitchen, she rinsed the cups and left them in the sink. She dawdled for a minute while she worried over what he *might* say and what she *should* say. Then she squared her shoulders and her resolve, and returned to the living room. She found Hunter staring pensively into the flickering flames.

He smiled up at her when she stopped near him, then he moved over to make a place for her to sit on the sofa between him and the fire. She sat in the corner with her feet drawn up under her borrowed robe.

Hunter spoke first. "After I saw Coop and the doctor, I stopped by the Sheriff's Office. I told them about your pictures, and they'll develop the film and document the photos. Of course, they'll return the other pictures to you, and I brought your camera back with me."

"I hope the photos will help convict them, Hunter. Will I have to testify?"

"Perhaps. It depends on whether they fight the charges. The sheriff seems to think they'll confess. At least Carney seems prone to admit his involvement. Then you may not have to appear in court."

"I'll do it, if it's necessary. I was scared up there in the mountains, and I'm certainly glad they didn't see me. But I was so angry with them too. To betray your trust like that and to leave Coop for dead." She balled her hands into small fists and sputtered, "I—I could have just *cussed!*"

Hunter laughed heartily. "My Lord, Hannah, I can't imagine cuss words crossing your lips, but if they ever do, I hope I'm there to hear it!"

It was Hannah's turn to laugh. "I probably wouldn't be very good at it."

"Oh, you never know!" he teased. Then, seriously, "I can't tell you how scared I was myself when I saw Pike with Coop's horse. I couldn't imagine Coop losing his horse as Pike claimed. I didn't want to, but it was hard not to think the worst. I kept seeing Coop lying somewhere in the snow."

"Me too, Hunter. I hadn't heard a shot, but I kept imagining him injured. When he gained consciousness, I wanted to ask him a lot of questions, but I also knew he should stay as quiet as possible. He was in a lot of pain." Hannah shifted on the sofa, turning a little toward him. "How did Coop run into the rustlers?"

"I'm afraid he'd done just what I'd asked the three younger guys not to do. He'd gone off alone looking for suspicious activity. Today, he'd gone up past the three springs, then in a roundabout way ridden down into that coulee. The one you saw from above several hours later. He said that he hadn't been there all summer, so he decided to give it a good look. He spotted an edge of that metal gate."

"Ahh . . . so that's why he entered that box canyon."

Hannah didn't protest when Hunter casually laid his left arm behind her on the back of the sofa and snuggled her close. She could feel the vibration of his voice where the top of her head touched his throat. It was a comfortable, connected feeling. She watched the fire and listened as Hunter continued Coop's story.

"He said he opened the gate just enough to ride through, then pulled it closed again. Of course, he saw the cattle and knew someone had deliberately hidden them there. He just didn't know who had, for sure anyway. He rode around the box canyon a bit, enough to know those cattle weren't the only ones who'd been there these last few months."

"You mean the rustlers hid cattle from your neighbor's ranches there too? That was pretty daring."

"Coop and I are sure they did. In fact, Ike told me earlier that a couple of Chuck Carson's Herefords were mixed in with mine in that truck they unloaded this afternoon."

"My goodness. I remember one of them saying they'd found a 'sweet little set-up' here."

"Yes, they had a good set-up, all right. A perfect box canyon with good grass and water and easy to close off. Far enough from the main herd but near enough to an access road to load them easily too, when the time was right. I suspect this would have been their last load for the season, as Pike knew I was thinking of moving them back to the ranch in a few days."

"Leaving Coop like that was a horrible thing to do!" she declared.

"You're right. Coop is sure to be laid up with that injured leg for a good while."

Hannah frowned. "Does he have somewhere to go while he recuperates? Family anywhere?"

"No, he's alone in the world, but we'll take care of him. He can stay here in the house, or if he prefers, down at the bunkhouse."

Hunter paused for a moment, and they sat quietly. He heard her audible sigh.

Then, "What are you thinking about, Hannah?"

She turned a little and saw his smile. It gave her the courage to say, "It's just that I'm not sure what's happening to us, Hunter."

"Maybe I know. You wanted time to get over an old romance, and I've tried my best to give you that necessary time. But these past few months, well, I've grown very fond of you. Getting to know you, working with you at school, our weekly rides, sharing a meal. It's just been great."

"I'm so surprised to hear you say that, Hunter. I like you very much, and all the things we've done together have been wonderful for me, too. But I didn't know if it meant as much to you."

Hunter replied soberly, "Well, I guess we agree that we like each other's company."

Hannah nodded. "Yes, that's true."

"I'm curious. Why did you really ride up to the falls today? I know about taking pictures, but up there with Coop you said something about wanting to be alone. What was troubling you, Hannah?"

She clasped her hands in her lap and breathed deeply. *If I'm going to tell him, now's the time!*

"I—I had a letter from my younger sister, Heidi, yesterday. I needed to digest it and make a decision. You see, I told you only part of my problem with Gregg Novak, my school principal. Heidi and he are planning a December wedding in Topeka."

Hunter reacted in surprise. "What? That's a shocker all right. Did you have any prior warning of it?" Hunter took her hand in his and held it gently.

"Yes, I did, so I shouldn't have been so upset. After I had time to think about it, I really wasn't upset anymore."

"Well, I'm glad to hear that. Do you want to tell me more?"

Hannah turned toward him. "Yes, I do." She went back to her childhood and covered happy times and sad. She explained how different Heidi and she were in appearance, personality, interests. She bared her soul about how socially inferior Heidi made her feel. She related how her sister always lured away any fellow interested in her.

"Is that what happened with this Gregg? Heidi got her hooks into him?"

"Yes, but please, don't think too badly of her. I honestly don't think she realizes how easily she turns men's heads." She added in an awed tone, "She's beautiful."

"So are you, Hannah," Hunter murmured quietly.

She ducked her head and stared at her lap. "No, I'm not. I'm plain . . . but, I try to do the best with what God gave me."

Hunter gently took her face between his hands. "Look at me, Hannah. You *are* a beautiful woman. You're lovely, warm, caring and giving. I think I'm falling in love with you. Very much in love. I fought against it at first. I was afraid of repeating past mistakes, but believe me, Hannah, you grew on me. I hadn't fully realized how much until tonight when I sat down across from you at the table. I was struck with the thought that I wanted to do that for the rest of my life."

"Oh, Hunter," she said, the words trembling on her lips. "How sweet you are. I—I thought perhaps the kisses today were just relief at finding Coop and me alive or something like that. I'd hoped but hadn't really believed that you could ever love me."

"Please believe me, Hannah." He kissed her forehead to emphasize his words.

"I've been regretting saying that I wasn't interested in a romantic involvement while I'm living here. But today, up at the waterfall, I decided to go to my sister's wedding. It would be a closure of sorts on the past." She looked shyly away. "In my heart, I hoped, truly hoped that someday you'd want me, too."

"I do, sweetheart, I do." He pulled her closer and kissed her soft lips. Hannah returned his kiss, then she pulled back. They both had tasted the residue of cocoa. Hunter's eyes gleamed as he said, "Chocolate!" Hannah and he smiled in remembrance of the afternoon's chocolate bar kisses.

Hunter took one of her hands in his and squeezed it gently. They sat quietly for awhile watching the flames slowly die down, before Hannah spoke again.

"I really like Elizabeth, Hunter. She's more the kind of

mother I would've hoped to have. I love my own, but she's so like Heidi in her personality. I guess I'm more like my father, and I still feel close to him. He's a good man, and he understood the pain I was feeling last spring when Gregg and Heidi fell in love. He supported my decision to move away from Topeka."

"I'm so glad that he did. I'll look forward to meeting him one day. The rest of your family too, especially your grandmother. She seems to be a very special lady."

"That she is," Hannah agreed whole-heartedly. "She's many things to me all rolled up into one wonderful person. I'd love for you to get to know her."

"I hope I get the opportunity."

"I was wondering," she began slowly, "what you meant about fighting against your attraction to me early on, and then you said you didn't want to repeat past mistakes. May I ask you to explain, Hunter; if you'd like, that is?"

He rubbed his free hand over his jaws for a moment, something Hannah had noticed him doing often over the past months. A habit when thinking, she supposed.

"Yes, I'll explain. It's only fair after your confiding in me about your sister and Gregg. I thought I was in love once. I guess it's been five or so years ago now, and it didn't work out. Cathy was a talented singer/songwriter who hoped to make it big one day. In the meantime, she was working in Bozeman as a waitress to support herself and taking any opportunity to perform in the area that she could find. Well, to make a long story short, I was smitten, but I had the good sense to invite her out to the ranch for a visit. I fully intended to ask her to marry me, if she liked the ranching life. So I guess it was a kind of test."

He paused, and Hannah asked, "Did she like it out here?"

"Oh, some. She liked to ride. She was interested in the cattle, mainly what price they could bring, and so forth. Do you get the picture?"

"I'm afraid I do," she murmured with a sad shake of her head.

"So, after a week or so, I came in one afternoon to find she'd packed her bags and was gone. She'd left a letter in my room. The gist of it was that she liked me, but she didn't love me. Not enough to bury herself out in the middle of nowhere, as she called this place. She wanted her career more, and she was determined to make it as a recording artist. She was on her way to Nashville, and by the way, thanks for the cash to get her there. She said she'd pay me back someday."

"Hunter! She stole from you?" Hannah was astonished. "Has she ever paid it back?"

"No. I've never heard from her. She cleaned out the wallet that I'd left on my dresser. I often don't take it with me while I'm out on the range, but at least she didn't take my credit cards. She also must have searched through my things as six hundred dollars was missing from a box in a drawer. I'd sold a filly that week and, foolishly, hadn't deposited the money yet. Too distracted by Cathy's visit, I suppose."

"Oh, Hunter dear, I'm so sorry all that happened to you. But I think this answers my question about your being wary of me at first. I'm certainly glad that you don't think I'm anything like that girl. You don't, do you?" She looked suddenly concerned that he could.

"No, not at all, Hannah, especially now that I know you so much better. I was just trying to protect myself against making a mistake again. It hurt at the time. I felt so foolish that I didn't even call the sheriff or tell Mom about the missing cash. Embarrassed, I guess. Too much male pride."

"Well, maybe, but things like that *do* hurt. It's hard to be let down by someone you care about," Hannah commented wisely. "I won't betray your confidence, Hunter. We won't talk of her or of Gregg again. Though since he'll be my brother-in-law, I'll have to see him occasionally."

"That's true, but we can handle that together. Thank you, Hannah, for listening to me and for understanding."

"You're very welcome." She laid her head back against his comfortable shoulder and sighed. He had said "together." That sounded so incredibly wonderful to Hannah.

"You know, your mother and I have had some pleasant visits. The day she and I rode together, we sat and talked for awhile. She told me about what happened with your younger brother, and then your father. I'm so sorry, Hunter. That had to have been a terribly difficult time for you."

He shrugged. "It was, that's for sure. But, it's a rare family that doesn't have some hard times in its history. We've done our best. Mom's a strong woman, and I've tried to manage the ranch in the way I felt Dad would have." He paused and shifted on the sofa as he put his feet up onto the coffeetable. "This fiasco with Pike and the men hasn't been a good example of managing the ranch, I'm afraid."

"Now, don't blame yourself for Pike. He and the others were targetting all the surrounding ranches too. Any of the other ranchers could have been the one to hire him."

Hunter hugged her. "Thanks for those kind words. Now, you've had a difficult time yourself with your family relationships and all, but you've come through it a sweet, compassionate woman. You're brave and full of heart."

"What a nice compliment, Hunter. I'd like to think it's true, but I know how I can quake inside at times. Perhaps Cinnamon is the one that's brave and full of heart. By the way, how's she doing?"

"Just fine. Ike checked her over, and her leg's showing no ill effects from the extra running today."

Hannah breathed a sigh of relief. "Good. I'd hoped so. She's such an outstanding horse."

Hunter murmured his agreement. They each smiled happily, and Hannah gave him a brief hug.

Hunter then remarked, "I'm really looking forward to the

rest of the school year. I know we'll both be busy, but there are so many places I want to take you. There's a couple of fine museums in Bozeman . . . you remember my love of history? Just up the road from Turk is the territorial capital that's being restored. It's a great spot to spend a day."

"That sounds like fun. I'm something of a history buff, too. What else?" she asked with a happy lilt in her voice.

"Have you ever seen a rodeo in person? There'll be a major rodeo and livestock show held in Billings in a few months. That would be a fun trip for you, and you could see our 'big city'."

"Oh, let's do that, Hunter."

"Okay, honey. Now that we're having our first snowfall of the season, the ski resorts will be opening for business by Thanksgiving. Would you be interested in that?"

"Well, yes, but I've never skied. Kansas is pretty flat, you know," she replied with a chuckle.

"No problem. We can start slow. I can even give you some lessons here before we try the slopes."

"Oh, yes! I remember you told me about skiing across the pastures to school. I'll look forward to learning."

"Good. It'll be a lot of fun."

They were quiet for a bit, then Hannah said, "I can hardly believe we're talking like this. Just this morning on my ride, I was wondering how you might react if I said I wanted to take back that earlier statement of 'no romantic involvement' while I was living here."

Hunter responded with a hoot of laughter, then kissed her soundly.

"That's how I'd react, my darling Hannah!"

She laughed and hugged him again, then leaned back and smiled into his hazel eyes. Then she asked something that attested to how confident and comfortable she felt with their new relationship.

"I do hope that all these plans aren't just because you and the School Board don't relish searching for a new teacher for next year?" she suggested teasingly, her head tilted to one side.

His eyes dancing, Hunter feigned serious consideration of her question.

"Well now, that *would* be a definite advantage, wouldn't it? Hm-mm." He rubbed a hand over his jaw. "And I'm sure that the other members of the board would be very pleased to be relieved of that duty. Not to mention your students who'd be happy to have you stay, I'm sure. Then there are the people in the community. I figure they'd like to have you around for more than one year. I know Ike, Cookie and the cowhands would be tickled pink. As for my mother," he chuckled deep in his throat, "she's probably hoping you'll stay in Whetstone permanently. I know she likes you very much. As for me . . . well, I vote for a permanent stay of about fifty or sixty years, if we're lucky."

Hannah's face glowed. "Well, I certainly can't disappoint that many people, can I?"

Epilogue

Pike, Skinny, and Carney finally admitted their guilt and were sentenced to prison time. They were fortunate. A century or so ago, they would have been hanged from the nearest tree. Rustling was not an offense taken lightly in the Old West.

Hunter accompanied Hannah when she flew to Topeka over Christmas break. Heidi's wedding to Gregg was a lovely ceremony. Hunter and Hannah's father became well-acquainted, and he loved Grandma Withers on sight.

Coop's broken leg healed slowly, but by spring he was back in the saddle. He was proud to take over as foreman of the Big G when Hunter offered the job.

The school year sped by. It was filled with study, activities, and fun times. The students' outdoor science lab notebooks were crammed by the end of May. The School Board, Hannah, and the other students presented a graduation program to honor their lone eighth-grader, Charlie.

Hannah was offered a new contract for the next school term, which she happily signed.

Elizabeth was thrilled that Hunter had found love. She set about making small changes in the house. She stored away some of her things, so that Hannah would have space to display favorite objects, such as Grandma Withers' clock and candlesticks. The major change was when she moved to a downstairs bedroom. She felt that Hunter should have the use of the master bedroom and would perhaps want to redecorate.

So, on a fine Saturday near the end of June, under a wide, blue Montana sky, the good people of Whetstone gathered at the little white church to witness and rejoice in the marriage of Hannah Morgan and Hunter Grissom. Hannah was delighted that her parents, her grandma, and her sister and brother-in-law had flown out for the ceremony.

Later that night, Hannah laid her head on Hunter's broad shoulder and thought she had never known such happiness in the whole of her life. She'd found her place in the world with this wonderful man, on this beautiful ranch, and in that little one-room school.

Hannah was home.